# A TIME TO LOVE

## TO THE TIME OF THE HIGHLANDERS
### BOOK TWO

ELLIE ST. CLAIR

## CONTENTS

| | |
|---|---|
| Prologue | 1 |
| Chapter 1 | 5 |
| Chapter 2 | 11 |
| Chapter 3 | 17 |
| Chapter 4 | 25 |
| Chapter 5 | 32 |
| Chapter 6 | 40 |
| Chapter 7 | 48 |
| Chapter 8 | 56 |
| Chapter 9 | 64 |
| Chapter 10 | 71 |
| Chapter 11 | 77 |
| Chapter 12 | 87 |
| Chapter 13 | 94 |
| Chapter 14 | 100 |
| Chapter 15 | 110 |
| Chapter 16 | 117 |
| Chapter 17 | 125 |
| Epilogue | 135 |
| An excerpt from A Time to Dream | 141 |
| *Also by Ellie St. Clair* | 147 |
| *About the Author* | 151 |

♥ **Copyright 2022 Ellie St Clair**

**All rights reserved.**

This book or parts thereof may not be reproduced in any form, stored in any retrieval system, or transmitted in any form by any means—electronic, mechanical, photocopy, recording, or otherwise—without prior written permission of the publisher.

Facebook: Ellie St. Clair

Cover by AJF Designs

Do you love historical romance? Receive access to a free ebook, as well as exclusive content such as giveaways, contests, freebies and advance notice of pre-orders through my mailing list!

Sign up here!

*To the Time of the Highlanders*
A Time to Wed
A Time to Love
A Time to Dream

For a full list of all of Ellie's books, please see
www.elliestclair.com/books.

# PROLOGUE

**Present Day - New York City**

"Bryan! Bryan? Where are you? I have the most amazing news!"

Emilia shrugged off her coat and threw it over the stuffed armchair as she kicked shut the door of the apartment she shared with her boyfriend of eight years. She had picked up the phone to call him from the university, but had then decided that this was news worthy of sharing in person. She could hardly wait to see his face when she told him. It wasn't often the unflappable Bryan showed much surprise, but this would be one accomplishment even he wouldn't be able to help but appreciate.

She had just started down the hallway when he shuffled out of the second bedroom that also served as his office. He ran a hand through his ruffled hair, his hazel eyes drooping with sleep deprivation. Clearly, he had been deep in research of philosophers of old.

"Bryan!" she said, practically skipping toward him. "I have the most amazing news."

"What time is it?" he asked, somewhat dazed. A professor

of philosophy, once he focused on something, it was often difficult to pull him out of it.

"Noon," she replied. "I just had to come home and tell you. You are looking at the new Professor of Scottish History at New York University!"

"What?" he said, his eyes suddenly clearing as he stared at her. "You?"

"Yes, me," she said, the grin affixed to her face. "The Dean personally invited me to his office this morning. He interviewed me on the spot, and said he couldn't think of anyone else who Dr. Brandt would want taking over his legacy. I still can't believe he's gone but it's… it's such an honor. Can you believe it?"

"No," he said perplexedly, shaking his head. "I can't. You're so young and inexperienced. Why would they give it to you?"

Her euphoric mood began to evaporate. She tried to tell herself that Bryan was just being Bryan — he always said exactly what he thought, never one to hold back. Usually Emilia appreciated that about him, but there were moments his candor could have been sugarcoated. Like right now, when she could use a little celebration.

"You know I worked under Dr. Brandt for nearly a decade," she said. "I owe my entire understanding of teaching to him, and he taught me everything I know about the Scottish Highlands. As far as I am aware, no other academic has ever focused so heavily on the 16th century and the day-to-day routines of the Highlanders. Not only that, but I understood his passion, Bryan. I can *feel* the people we research, their desperation to save their lives, their families, and their heritage. I *understand* the importance of the wars based around clans and their family honor. The Dean didn't think there would be anyone else who could step into Dr. Brandt's shoes and take over his courses and his research where he had so unexpectedly left them."

Bryan leaned into the doorjamb.

"Listen, Emilia, you know I feel badly about Dr. Brandt," said Bryan of the man who had died of a brain tumor just four months ago. "He was an amazing man, and you had such a bond with him. Do you think maybe, though, you're jumping into this because of your grief? You were so close to him, perhaps you just need some time—"

"Are you not happy for me?" she demanded, crossing her arms over her chest. "Bryan, this is everything I ever dreamed of! I wish I had achieved this after his retirement instead of his death, but is it not better me than someone else?"

"I know, Emilia, and honestly, I don't really understand your fascination with it all — brutes dressed in kilts, playing bagpipes, carrying their large swords into barbaric and unnecessary wars. But you love it, and so that's what matters. I'm just wondering if you maybe want to take some time and make sure it's what you really want, and not just what Dr. Brandt wanted for you?"

Emilia counted to ten as she silently fumed. What Bryan saw as "barbaric" was, to her, an important and specific part of history and culture. True, war was messy, but it was important to understand the context and the circumstances leading to and resulting from it.

This was not a new argument. Emilia and Bryan had bonded in their first years of college over their love of books and aversion to beer-drinking social activities. Emilia always found Bryan's constant search for knowledge sexy and mysterious. Over time, however, she had begun to feel an uneasy yearning for something more. What had once been fun and exciting had become, as much as she hated to admit it, a friendship more than anything else, while their passions lay elsewhere. In this, however, she had expected his support.

"Look, Bryan, I can't begin to understand your obsession with the writings of Plato and Aristotle, and all of the other philosophers that fill your mind. But I don't question it, nor do I question your dreams."

Which, she suddenly realized, was likely the root of this. Bryan had been working for years to achieve tenure. True, his colleagues found his application of the works of the great philosophers on everyday life somewhat genius, but so far that hadn't amounted into any permanent placement. And now she had achieved it so quickly. It made some sense why he was being so unsupportive.

"Bryan," she said slowly. "I realize you may be upset right now — jealous even. But I am your partner here, and I need you to be happy for me."

"I am," he said, though the frown didn't leave his face. "I just think you should really consider this before moving forward."

"You know what?" she said, the words coming out before she could even process what she was saying, as if her subconscious decided it needed to act before she overanalyzed this. "You're right."

"Good," he said, pushing himself away from the wall and starting back down the hall to his office. "I'm glad you've seen reason."

"I have," she said in measured tones, her voice drifting down the hallway and through the door to his ears. "In fact, I am moving forward, Bryan. I'm moving out. We're done here."

## CHAPTER 1

PRESENT DAY

The sky was gray as Emilia hefted her heavy bag out of the cab and began rolling through the sliding glass doors of the JFK Airport.

She pushed her way through the typical New York City crowd, anxious to find her gate and be on her way.

Her phone dinged, and she stopped for a moment to check it, smiling when she saw that it was the Dean of History wishing her safe travels. She had been so grateful he had allowed her a couple of weeks' vacation before she assumed her new position. She knew it was a strange time to travel when she had so much to prepare for, but she had been itching to visit the land she had studied for so long, and now that she had broken things off with Bryan, she felt somewhat… free.

Emilia had moved her belongings out the day after she told him about her new job, and was staying in a friend's spare bedroom until she could find a decent apartment close to work. She still cared for Bryan as a friend, but this new step forward in her life was the opportunity she needed to force herself to admit that he wasn't the love of her life. The fact that her tears had been few and her heart free instead of heavy confirmed the truth of it.

She found her gate to Aberdeenshire, Scotland, where she would fly into before taking a taxi to Stonehaven. It had been her dream destination for years and she used to stare at the pictures online, wishing her life had been centered in that port city instead of the streaming metropolis around her. She couldn't wait to stand among the remains of old castles looking out over the ocean on the famous cliffs of Scotland. It was definitely better than scouring New York real estate to find somewhere she could afford while trying to ignore Bryan and his constant nagging to move out the remainder of her belongings.

She just couldn't deal with real life right now, and the only thing she felt like doing at the moment was leaving it all behind to visit the place where some of her ancestors had roamed, see the battlefields of the warring clans, and disappear from life for a bit into the world of her studies.

"Flight 6780 to Aberdeen, Scotland will be boarding in five minutes. Please have your tickets ready and your carry-on luggage tagged appropriately," the voice cracked over the speaker.

Emilia gathered her bag and purse and stood, walking over to the gathering crowd and waiting for them to call her section. She had already been through two security checks so she knew her bag was approved. All she really wanted to do was get into her seat, have a glass of whiskey, and relax. Boarding went quickly since the flight wasn't all that full, and Emilia strapped herself into her window seat, shoving her purse under the seat in front of her and taking a deep breath.

"Well, hello," a nasally voice said from the aisle seat across the empty middle.

"Hi," Emilia replied, smiling at the very loudly dressed woman.

She was strange in a way Emilia couldn't quite put her finger on. Her hair was as red as Emilia's, but frizzy and wild, partially pulled back in a bun. She was wearing black-rimmed glasses, a bright multi-colored sweater, and didn't seem to be carrying anything, not even a purse. She smiled kindly as she sat rigidly and buckled up, leaning her head back against the seat with a nervous look in her eye. As the plane took off, she clasped the handles of her seat and Emilia turned toward the window, chastising herself for staring.

She could remember the first time she had ever flown. It was with her grandmother and they had, oddly enough, been visiting Scotland. For over a month, Emilia and her grandmother had traveled all across the country. That was when Emilia really started becoming interested in history, specifically Scottish history. Little did she know the trip was all a means to distract her eleven-year-old self from her parents' pending divorce. When she returned home, she dove into history, collecting all the books she could get her hands on, ignoring the drama going on around her.

As soon as the flight was in the air, Emilia ordered a double whiskey, threw in her headphones to avoid any awkward conversations, and zoned out. She watched as the plane traveled high over the ocean, everything below appearing so tiny and insignificant. She listened to a couple of songs on her playlist and then pulled out her laptop, deciding between a few old movies that she usually enjoyed. She finally chose *Grease*, her guilty pleasure. Another glass of whiskey later, she was fighting sleep. When the lights dimmed in the cabin and the sun outside of her window finished setting, it was game over. Emilia had been up for days, too worried and anxious about life to really sleep. But now, when relaxing was her only option, her body took over, and into the dream world she went.

Her dreams were wild, and oddly, the frazzled redheaded woman beside her was in all of them. Emilia was traveling through some kind of portal and everything was black. She couldn't see or hear anything except the woman's voice, which kept repeating over and over again, "Listen to your heart." After what seemed like hours, Emilia could see a light approaching on the other end of the tunnel and as her feet touched down on the soft grass, she found herself in a very familiar Scotland, one she had studied for decades. Before she could look around or ask any questions, she was jolted awake by the landing of the plane.

Emilia squinted her eyes, trying to see around her, but she wasn't quite ready for the brightness of the sun shining through the window. She took a deep breath and looked beside her, but the seat was empty. She furrowed her brow and looked up and down the aisle, but the woman with red hair seemed to have just vanished. She thought about asking a flight attendant where the woman had gone, but by the time any of them were out of their seats, they were pulling up to the gate. Emilia shrugged her shoulders and pulled her carry-on out of the overhead hold before walking slowly out of the plane. While she waited for her luggage, she looked around for the woman, but she was still nowhere to be seen. Strange.

Emilia collected her bags and headed out to find a car to take her to Stonehaven. Luckily, there were several taxis waiting out front, so she hopped in one and gave the address to the cottage she had rented by the ports. As the cab pulled out, she glanced over, startled to find her eyes lock with the mysterious woman from the plane. She was the only figure standing still amongst the moving crowd, smiling at Emilia as she passed in the taxi, as if she was there specifically to watch her. Emilia shook her head, figuring she must be going crazy, and decided it was better to focus on getting settled than on this strange woman.

The drive was relaxing, and she completely forgot all about her worries as she passed through the beautiful rolling hills of Stonehaven. Off in the distance to her right peaked mountains that rose toward the sky, and to her left the beautiful ocean glittered like diamonds. Peace finally settled over her, and she sat back with a sigh of contentment, knowing she had made the right decision to come here. This trip would be everything she needed to feel like herself again.

When Emilia arrived at the cottage, she was almost giddy as she dragged her bags inside and left them in the entryway. She was too excited to worry about unpacking at the moment and immediately grabbed her notepad and set up her laptop.

Emilia was a planner, and she wanted to schedule every single moment of her trip to make sure she was able to really see everything she yearned to explore. There were more castles, remains, historical sites, and libraries on her list to visit than she could fit on one page.

She had two weeks but she didn't even think that would be enough time to really take in everything and still get a good sleep every night. She was like a kid on Christmas morning, unable to unwrap an unending pile of presents.

Emilia lit the fireplace to ward off the chill of the Scottish evenings and went through the cupboards to see what the cottage owners had stocked the kitchen with. She was pleased to find everything she had required, plus a ton of traditional Scottish dishes. One thing was certain, she definitely wouldn't go hungry while she was here. After making a warm cup of tea, she sat down in front of her laptop, staring at the pictures of Dunnottar Castle on the cliffs of Stonehaven. It was going to be her first castle tour, and she couldn't wait to see what her visit would reveal about its history.

## CHAPTER 2

1545 ~ STONEHAVEN, SCOTLAND

"*Oh, roe, soon shall I see them, oh,*
    *Hee-roe, see them, oh see them.*
*Oh, roe, soon shall I see them,*
*the mist covered mountains of home!*
*There shall I visit the place of my birth.*
*They'll give me a welcome the warmest on earth.*
*So loving and kind, full of music and mirth,*
*the sweet sounding language of home..."*

THE MEN WERE in good spirits, singing their songs and eating their supper, waiting for the first morning light to creep over the horizon. The mist laid low in the darkness of the night and though Dougal wanted to join in with the lads, he knew that he was better to maintain a solemn, stoic silence. They had arrived right before dusk to the fields beyond Dunnottar Castle on the cliffs.

When the sun began to rise, they would meet their warring clan, the Buchanans, in an effort to keep them from trying to steal their lands and marry their women. The Buchanans were an angry, though wealthy clan. Dougal knew they were convinced that coin could buy them the best beasts for battle and were certain of victory. Dougal knew better than anyone, however, that it was heart that won these battles, not the amount spent on swords. And heart was definitely something of which the MacGavin clan had plenty.

"Brother," Ivor said, greeting Dougal and setting his plate down on the ground as he dislodged his sword and sat next to him. "Yer awful quiet over here by yerself."

"Just thinking," Dougal replied. "'Tis a lot to be mulling over tonight."

"'Not like you, to be so caught up in affairs outside the coming battle," Ivor said, looking over at him. "Can I help ye any?"

"Since me father died, years ago, I knew my place would be as Laird when I came of age," Dougal said, pushing around the oatcakes on his plate. "When they made my uncle the Master of the House to watch over the clan until I reached that point, I didna realize it would eventually become a struggle for power. It's nigh time I took my place as true leader of this clan."

"The elders want ye there, though, do they not?"

"I suppose," Dougal said shrugging. "They must be aware just how dedicated I am to the clan, and how I am ready to take my rightful place."

"I am sure they already know that," Ivor said, patting Dougal on the shoulder with his meaty palm. "But we are glad to be having ye out here. The Buchanans need to be shown just where they fit into this world."

"You mean under my boot heel?" They laughed hard then sat quietly listening as the men continued to sing their songs of war and life. Dougal had been in this very spot so many times as a child that he knew exactly what was around him, even if the moon was clouded over and the night was darker than usual.

The castle was held by a friendly clan, the Keiths, who had agreed to allow the MacGavins to pass through their land to the nearby empty fields as they waited for the Buchanans.

The lights from the far-off castle glimmered in the distance. Dougal and Ivor were, however, more focused on the mountains, over which the Buchanans would be coming. They were across the empty flowing fields and deep in the mist, where no one had yet to build or farm. The land's ownership was up for debate. The MacGavins had heard of the Buchanans' plans to raid their lands, and decided to head them off before they reached their own holdings.

Dougal finished his food and nodded at Ivor, glad to have his closest friend there with him. He had spent so much time taking care of the lands and the family that he hadn't forged the type of bond with most of the other men that he would prefer.

Still, they looked to Dougal in times of battle, as his uncle was now too old to involve himself in these affairs. Dougal had been only ten years of age when his father battled against this same Buchanan clan, losing his life with a swift blow to the gut. He was brought back to his home and tended to, with Dougal by his side, until he took his last breath. Dougal would never forget the day when they laid him to rest in the fields beyond their land. His father had been a strong warrior and believed in the days of old when the laird protected the people, and the other clans stayed quietly in their own lands.

As the days had progressed, however, famine and drought had come down hard on their soil and they were left trading sheep and farming what was left of the dry land. Dougal's mother had died of fever, or as some believed a broken heart, soon after his father, and his uncle had been named Master of the MacGavins until Dougal was ready to assume the position. His uncle had been a weak leader, leaving many of the decisions to the elders.

As Dougal grew older, he'd started to take more of a leading role, and now he was determined to show the elders he was more than their most skilled warrior. He had heard a whisper of it in the winds recently and knew that this battle would be the moment in which he could prove to them he was ready.

Dougal stood up from the ground and stretched before pulling on his sword. Ivor stood beside him and strode toward the fires, pulling his deerskin cloak over his shoulders for warmth. The men stood in reverence as Ivor passed, having seen him fight in battles before.

Dougal had spent many years training and readying himself for skirmishes like this, and his skills had proven to bring a great deal of confidence to the men of his clan. He may not be a mighty speaker, but he could yield a sword better than most, a talent highly sought after and respected in a prospective laird.

Dougal walked past the broods of warriors and toward the tents set up for sleeping. He looked up at the starry sky and watched as several clouds passed over, dimming the moon's light. He didn't quite know why he felt it, but there was definitely a strangeness in the air that was bothering him. Everything seemed just a little off, and it didn't make him feel confident in the battle ahead of him.

Still, he looked over at his trained men and knew that the Buchanans stood little chance against them. Dougal wasn't ready to lose men in war, but it was always inevitable. He hoped his own last days were still a long way off, as his sister would be left without anyone to care for her, and the clan left without an heir.

Which was yet another omission on his part to this point in his life.

Dougal walked straight past his tent and out into the field, pulling out his sword and beginning to thrust it through the cool night air. His muscles were tense as anticipation built in his stomach and radiated out to the rest of him.

Times were changing for Dougal's country. Scotland had found themselves being ruled by their first queen without a king by her side. Where once clans were content with maintaining their lands, now many were becoming bolder, looking to take what wasn't theirs. The MacGavins preferred to keep things as they were, to be left alone to raise their young, farm their fields, and make it through this troubled time when Scotland was more concerned about England, leaving the Highlanders to fend for themselves. Dougal didn't mind the battles, but hated returning home to tell a wife or mother she had lost a husband or son. The Buchanans, however, had been a thorn in the MacGavins' side for far too long. Dougal had a personal vendetta against the Buchanan who had killed his father, making this day even more important to him.

Dougal swung his sword until sweat beaded up on his forehead. The cold wind from the ocean hit those drops and sent shivers down his spine. Dougal put his sword back into its sheath and headed toward his tent, for rest at least, even if sleep evaded him. His body needed to be strong, energized, and ready when the battle began.

Dougal pulled back the flap covering his tent door and stepped inside, finding the pile made up for him on the ground, covered in furs and pillows. The men knew Dougal liked to sleep on the ground like the rest of them, but continued to do as they had for his uncle, making it as comfortable as possible inside his tent. Dougal did welcome the sign of respect, and truth be told he would not argue with a bit of comfort every once in a while, especially the night before an important battle.

The Buchanans had picked a fight over the grazing territory for sheep. Dougal had met with the clan's leader, but Laird Alastair Buchanan had not seemed interested in finding a compromise. Dougal had been deeply scrutinized by the elders of his clan, and he knew this was about more than sheep for him.

Dougal collapsed onto the pillows, folding his arms behind his head as he thought about the battle tomorrow and his future beyond it. The knot in his stomach was still present, telling him that something out of the ordinary was about to happen, but like before, he could not pinpoint exactly what it would be.

He and his advisors knew the warring clan's number of men was slightly more than their own, although not as well trained. They knew the Buchanans had newly forged armor to shield them when fighting. All of this knowledge was from a Buchanan that brought them details, having had enough of Alastair's ways.

As the cold wind blew through the tent, allowing the deep singing voices of the men to penetrate its thin walls, Dougal prepared himself for the clash that would determine the fate of himself and his clan.

## CHAPTER 3

PRESENT DAY

*E*milia found the sun shining through the window both annoying and exciting. She was exhausted and jet lagged but didn't want to waste even one day while she was here. Dean Talbot had sat her down and told her to make sure she relaxed on this vacation, knowing full well that she would pack her holiday so full of exploration and education that she would need time to recover once she returned home.

As much as lounging around and sleeping half the day sounded enticing, she had specifically chosen this location over a typical beach trip knowing she wouldn't be spending her time relaxing in the sun, pondering her life. Even the weather was cooperating for a day of exploring the Scottish landscapes.

Emilia pulled herself out of bed and jumped in to the shower. The water was only lukewarm but she embraced it as it woke her up, helping her get a jump on the day. She pulled her long red hair back into a ponytail and dressed in comfortable walking clothes. Stonehaven wasn't a particularly large place but visiting without a car meant she would be doing a lot of exploration on her feet. Taxis were pretty expensive out here, and Emilia wanted to try to limit her time in them to the commute to the Stonehaven ports and back home at the end of the day. It would allow her the chance to take in the outdoors and enjoy the scenery the Highlands had to offer. As she reviewed the itinerary she had created for the day, her blood started pumping in excitement.

She headed down to the kitchen and set the pot of coffee to brew while she sat down with a bowl of yogurt and fresh berries. She went over the day's schedule once again, then folded it up and stuck it in her pocket. She had already packed her bag for the day, and added fruit and bread for an afternoon snack. Her plan was to spend the entire day in museums and libraries, leaving the castle tours and exploration for the next day.

The castles were what Emilia was really looking forward to, but she wanted to take her time in the library first, soaking up as much information about the area's history as she could through resources that might not have been available at home. Every place had those few little secrets that no one but the locals knew, and those were the stories Emilia wanted to hear.

She was drawn away from her thoughts by the sound of the taxi honking out front. She tossed her dishes in the sink and ran out with her backpack in tow. It was, surprisingly, the same man who had driven her to the cottage, and he smiled at her when she relayed her destination. Emilia had grown up the token nerd, and she remained the studious sort. People who met her the first time took in her slim build, wavy hair, and perfect skin and made assumptions. It wasn't until she started talking that they realized she wasn't what she seemed.

Emilia just couldn't understand how someone could live in a place and not know everything about its history. She supposed it was similar to the way she currently lived in New York City and had never taken a boat tour around the Statue of Liberty. Nothing is as exciting when it's home.

Through the day, Emilia found herself having to keep track of the time since she was losing herself in the history, the books, and the relics she discovered. Every place she visited had its own story, its own legends, and its own brutal battles through history. The largest of the libraries was so amazing she vowed to return another time while on this vacation to have the opportunity to see even more.

She pulled a huge stack of books from the shelves and sat at a table, skimming through them, discovering the secrets hidden in the Gaelic. There weren't very many people who actually spoke fluent Gaelic anymore, but once she had determined the nature of her studies, she had found it pertinent to learn the language to better understand the older texts. She was amazed — both shocked and saddened — at how much historians had missed due to poor translations.

As she was growing up, Emilia's father had been keen to keep the family's Scottish heritage alive, especially since Emilia's great-grandparents immigrated to America before her grandparents were born. Her family had taken a lot of time to make sure that their history was preserved. Guthrie was a fairly common surname throughout Scotland, but Emilia's family knew exactly where her great-grandparents had come from, so they had been able to track the family's place in history. They knew that Emilia's ancestors had been lairds to their clan for many decades. Emilia's mother's heritage was primarily Irish, the combination of ancestries apparent through Emilia's fiery red hair. The freckles dotting her nose and hazel eyes were pure Scottish.

When Emilia finished skimming through the last book

in her stack, she realized it was nearly lunch. Her stomach was grumbling and though she had brought food, she was craving some traditional Scottish cuisine. As Emilia was in the port city, there were more than enough choices for her to mull over. As the sign requested, she left the books in a stack on the table and headed out of the library and into the small city. She took her time casually wandering the streets, looking down at the old cobblestone walkways and imagining what it was like to walk these same stones ages ago.

Finally, her stomach led her to a small restaurant in the middle of the town, where she chose a table near the window. She could see the ocean's waves hitting the docks below, as fishermen moved throughout the town, bringing in their morning catches. Emilia could have sat there all day watching the people, but all the other historical museums were calling her name so she picked up the menu and began perusing.

It was traditional Scottish food, the menu much different from any café in the United States. She mulled the list over for several minutes before deciding on mince, tatties, a glass of water, and some whiskey. It was crazy to her how everywhere she went they sold whiskey. She half expected to see some for sale in the library.

She was now pleased her rumbling stomach had extracted her from the aisles and aisles of historical writings. She could have stayed there for days. Emilia pulled out her piece of paper and looked at her plan of action for the rest of the day. She was so absorbed in her list and her daydreams of what was to come that she didn't notice the person walking toward her until it was too late and she practically jumped with fright.

"Anyone sitting here?" The red-haired woman from the plane plopped herself down across from Emilia. Her hair was just as wild as before but this time she was wearing a plaid sweater adorned with cats.

"Hello," Emilia said, surprised. "I was beginning to think I had imagined you. What happened to you on the airplane?"

"That happens more than you know," the woman giggled, evading Emilia's question. "Let me introduce myself. I'm Fiona. Now tell me, what did you think of the Stonehaven Library?"

"It was so amazing," Emilia replied, smiling at the waitress as she set food down in front of her. "I literally could have stayed there all day. My name is Emilia. How did you know I was at the library?"

"Did you know that right where that library sits used to be several blacksmith shops?"

"Huh," Emilia replied, looking at her papers. "I didn't know that. I thought I had researched everything there was to find about this area."

"It was called Blacksmith Row and merchants would go there and have the blacksmiths bid on the services they needed," she said looking down at Emilia's mince and tatties, the expression on her face reminiscent. "You could get some really great work done for very little cost."

"That's so strange that there isn't any mention about that in anything I've read," Emilia said, shaking her head.

"In the mid-1500s this area went through a bit of scuffle," Fiona went on. "The church and state wanted to control the ports but because of the drought, the clans constantly butted heads with them."

"Drought? I wasn't aware of a drought," Emilia replied, intoxicated with this new information.

"It's not in any of your books," she smiled. "But I have a way to see the past."

"It seems you do," Emilia laughed, not sure if this woman was having her on right now or if she truly did have access to information not publicly available. Perhaps a private collection of books or journals. "I'd love a time machine right about now."

Fiona struck Emilia as so strange, yet she knew aspects of history that Emilia could neither confirm or deny. It was really odd, and Fiona was obviously a bit off her rocker, but Emilia didn't care. She enjoyed talking to her, and was used to people who were a bit different than the usual.

Fiona went on and on about unknown history of the area, pointing Emilia to different venues that she could check out, with directions to each as Emilia furiously noted down her tales and tips. None of the sites had been on Emilia's list, but they sounded so intriguing that she couldn't help but add them.

"Have you been to Dunnottar Castle yet?" Fiona asked.

"Mm," Emilia said, swallowing her food. "Not yet. I have it on my list for tomorrow."

"Tomorrow would be a perfect day to tour the ruins," Fiona said, wide eyed. "I would suggest going first thing when the sun rises. It's quite a spectacular view, and you never know who you'll meet along the path."

"Really? I'll do that then," Emilia said, putting a note next to the schedule. "I definitely want to see everything. I think tomorrow is actually the anniversary of the final MacGavin/Buchanan battle recorded. I was never satisfied with my research on their rivalry but now, with the information and background you've given me, I think I am starting to understand it a bit more."

"It's a fascinating story," Fiona said, leaning in. "The MacGavins just wanted to rule their lands, while the Buchanans wanted to take them over. They thought they were sly enough to make it about the sheep trade but the son of the MacGavin Laird saw right through it."

"You really know your history of the area," Emilia said,

cursing that she was unable to wait any longer. She asked Fiona, "would you mind waiting here while I run to the ladies' room? I'll just be a moment, I promise."

"Of course," Fiona chirped.

Emilia ran off to the restroom, thinking about the battle and what Fiona had said about being there at first light. While Emilia had been looking forward to sleeping in, she would wake up early for the sunrise. There was something about this woman that led Emilia to trust her advice — about history, at least. Emilia washed her hands and walked back out to the table, somehow unsurprised and yet disappointed to find an empty seat across from hers. As abruptly as she had arrived, Fiona had disappeared again, leaving Emilia wondering again if she was starting to lose it.

"Excuse me," she said quietly to the waitress. "Did you see where the red-haired woman went?"

"Sorry," the waitress replied. "I didn't even see another red-haired woman."

That was odd, thought Emilia. How had she not seen her? Fiona had been sitting there the entire time, including when the waitress had brought the food. Emilia thanked the waitress and paid for her meal before gathering her things and heading off to the Port Museum near the docks. She knew that there was so much for her to discover, but she couldn't shake the whole experience with Fiona from her mind, from the history she'd provided her to her strange appearances and disappearances.

To top it all off, whenever Emilia thought of the day to come, her stomach churned and she felt as if something earth shattering was lurking around the next corner. She pushed away the feeling and enjoyed the rest of her time in the port perusing the relics in the museums and gawking at the historical texts that the unique bookstores had on display.

At the end of the day, Emilia returned to the cottage and

grabbed a blanket, covering herself as she watched shooting stars jet across the night sky. Everything seemed so different here, as if she were in another world. Her mind drifted to her conversation with Fiona and her visit to the remains of the castle tomorrow. She felt pulled to it, like there was more there for her than stone ruins. She supposed she would have to wait and find out what was to come in the morning.

## CHAPTER 4

1545

The sky was beginning to lighten outside the tent as Dougal wrapped his kilt around himself and laced his boots. There had been no sign of the Buchanans just yet, but he knew they were coming.

He dressed in the rest of his gear and picked up his shield, holding it tightly in his hand and throwing his shoulders back, getting used to its weight. He stretched his legs and arms, loosening up for the impending battle. As he leaned over to touch his toes, giving his back a good solid stretch, a young clan member stuck his head inside the tent.

"Sorry to bother ye," he said. "But the elders are requesting a word with ye out in the fields."

"Thank you," Dougal nodded, standing back up and cracking his neck.

What would the elders want at this junction? They weren't here to fight, but would remain at the campsite, tending to the injured, and readying themselves for a quick departure. They would know he was currently preparing, mentally and physically, for the Buchanans' arrival. It made for a strange time to be requesting his presence. Dougal straightened his gear and stepped out of the tent, looking over at the rest of the men who had begun to rise. They were ready to transform from clan members to stealthy warriors, to protect their freedoms at all costs.

As Dougal stared out at the warriors, Ivor stepped out of the tent beside his. He fixed his twisted clothing and sheathed his sword, flexing his large chest and breathing deeply. He looked over at Dougal's lost gaze and hit him hard on the shoulder.

"Do ye not love that smell?"

"What smell?"

"The smell of cinders burning in the fire pits, the smell of porridge cooking, and most of all, the smell of battle looming in the distance," he said.

Ivor lived for these days, always preparing for battle, even when there wasn't one to be had. He worked with lumber and his build was gigantic. He stood at least four inches above Dougal, who was a tall man himself. But Ivor's size fooled people, for he was fast and ruthless when it came to battle. He was willing to do anything to protect the MacGavin clan, and Dougal was pretty sure he enjoyed severing a few heads now and then.

"Aye," Dougal laughed. "Well, I shall be over here. The elders want a word. Make sure the horns are sounded when the Buchanans arrive."

"The elders? On the mornin' of a battle?"

"Aye," Dougal grimaced. "I either did something very right or very wrong."

"Good luck, lad," Ivor said, shaking Dougal's hand. "And try to keep that temper for the battlefield."

Dougal nodded and watched as Ivor clomped out toward

the line of food that had been laid out. Dougal never ate on the morning of a battle, knowing that stopping because of a cramp or stomachache was sure to get him killed. He turned toward the field and watched as the four elders stood talking amongst themselves. They were dressed in their sashes and ribbons, pins depicting battles won in the past. Dougal suddenly became aware of his own presentation as he smoothed down his dark hair and repeated Ivor's words in his head. His friend was right. He needed to keep his head, especially during a time like this.

"Maidin," Dougal said in Gaelic as he approached. "Dúradh liom go raibh tú ag labhairt liomsa."

"Aye," the oldest responded, stepping forward. "It is true, we do wish to have a word with you."

"I hope you understand, with all due respect, it's moments before the battle begins," Dougal said, bowing his head.

"We willna keep ye long," Leonis, the oldest of the clan, replied. "We want you to know that we have been talking and we believe that when you win this battle, you will be ready to replace your uncle and take your rightful place as Laird of the MacGavin Clan."

"I had been hoping to hear that from ye soon," Dougal said, trying not to show too much excitement. "I would be honored to move forward as Laird."

"Good," Leonis said nodding his head.

"Well, if that will be all," Dougal replied, turning back toward the camp.

"Not quite," Leonis continued, raising a finger. "We need you to start looking for a wife. The Clan needs a lady next to their laird. Had you chosen one we would have made you Laird sooner, but ye have yet to find a woman and it's high time you took on this role."

"Ach," Dougal scoffed, trying not to be disrespectful but wondering how they were expecting him to take care of finding a wife while on the battlefields. He knew they were right, but now wasn't the time for such a discussion.

"We are serious," Leonis responded. "You need to be capable of producing an heir to the clan. We understand these battles are important, all the fighting in the world willna mean a thing if there is no one to take over when you are gone."

Dougal started as the trumpeter began to sound the alarm. The five of them turned and looked out over the field. Marching from the mist were the Buchanan warriors, their shields newly forged and strong, their swords sparkling in the rising sun. Dougal turned back to the elders and bowed to take his leave.

"Dougal," Leonis said stepping forward. "Remember that the most important thing beyond survival is the ability to birth children and create a long-lasting road of strength for this clan in the future."

"I will do my best," he said, understanding what they were saying but still wondering where he was going to immediately find a bride to appease their wishes. At the moment, he had more pressing issues, such as the troops who were rapidly approaching.

Dougal left the elders and headed toward Ivor, who he could see standing taller than all the others. As Dougal approached, Ivor looked at him with a devilish grin of excitement before turning to stare out toward the mountains. While the MacGavins were slightly outnumbered in men, they knew how to protect themselves and they knew that for every four ignorant warriors was one well-prepared MacGavin.

They watched as the Buchanans marched forward, flying their crests high in the sky. Alastair Buchanan led the charge and the approaching enemy walked to the center of the waving grasses, halting as their leader moved forward.

A TIME TO LOVE

Dougal took in a deep breath, knowing he was the one that would be meeting him.

"Ready the clan," he commanded Ivor, picking up his shield and walking out to meet Alastair.

The air was stagnant and everything was silent as he marched through the grasses toward the Buchanan Laird. Alastair smiled malevolently as Dougal approached, lowering his shield and sheathing his sword. Dougal knew there was no possible chance he was backing down from this fight but it was customary to attempt to resolve their grievances before sending their clans into battle. Alastair was the man who took Dougal's father's life so many years ago, and though his face was a bit more weathered, the strategist could still be seen shimmering in his eye.

"Ah, young Dougal," Alastair said as he stepped forward. "I hear they have not trusted your leadership just yet."

"Do you not think we are beyond battling over sheep, Buchanan?" he asked, ignoring the taunt.

"You know very well this ain't over any sheep," he replied, a serious look taking over.

"You canna have our lands," Dougal said fiercely.

"Then I suppose there is nothing more to talk about, is there?"

"I suppose not," he replied, watching as Alastair picked his shield back up and smiled.

"I shall make sure to take it easy on you," he laughed. "Not like I did on your daddy."

"By the end of this, I shall have your head on a spike," Dougal growled.

He turned and stormed back toward Ivor, his hand grasping the butt of his sword. He could see the excitement spark in Ivor's eyes as he glared out at the warring clan. Dougal stepped in front of his men, looking at each one of their faces. Some were older, from a generation when warring clans were few and far between, while others were young, fresh, and scared. It was up to him to ensure they were all prepared for what was to come.

"Men," Dougal said loudly. "We no longer bicker over petty things. We no longer fight for sheep or plow. Today, we fight for our lands, our homes, and our freedom! Hoist your swords and know that if you perish on this lofty soil, you will be remembered as a proud MacGavin warrior!"

They shouted and chanted as Dougal gathered his nerves and glanced over at the elders standing to the side. Leonis nodded at him approvingly as Dougal turned toward the field and lifted his sword high in the air. He took a deep breath and shouted the MacGavin battle cry.

"Luach agus bua!"

Valor and Victory.

The clan repeated their battle cry in a shout and took off across the field, clashing violently in the center with the Buchanans. Dougal was at the head of the brigade, slicing through warriors with his sword while watching his clansman closely. It was his responsibility to keep these men safe, and he would go to any extent to do so, even if that meant being first into the melee.

The MacGavins battled hard and strong, pushing their swords through the Buchanan clan, stepping over their bodies as they made headway through the droves of men behind them. Dougal looked up at the top of the hill and could see Alastair standing at the top, his shield down and his eyes watching every movement. It was a slap in the face to not have the laird facing him in battle, and anger simmered in his blood at the man's cowardice.

How dare he think he was so much better than them, that he could stand at the back and watch his men fight his battles for him. Dougal had seen this clan ravage farm houses and villages to the east and he would not allow them to do that to

MacGavin territory. His sister's face flashed through his mind as he roared loudly, clashing swords with a man in front of him.

The Buchanans seemed to have been working on their training, and Dougal noticed how hard his own men had to battle. Rage rippled through his chest as he watched one of his men fall before Ivor pulled a sword from a dead warrior and drove through the crowd yielding not one, but two blades. He was a beast of a fighter and he took no pity on the men in the field around him. He almost thrived on the blood spraying from their wounds as he crushed the warring clan with his might and anger.

Dougal lifted his shield, blocking a blow, watching as one of his men came up behind two Buchanan warriors and slit their throats. Dougal reached up and wiped the blood from his face, nodding at his clansman and moving forward. He wanted Alastair. He wanted to see him writhe in pain as he thrust his sword into his belly, knowing he would feel the same pain he had inflicted on his father so long ago. Dougal longed for that revenge, allowing it to drive him forward as Alastair scanned the crowd, his eyes settling on his adversary, a flash of fear crossing his face.

Dougal stepped forward, his eyes on Alastair as he moved to charge up the hill, when a searing pain blew through his shoulder. He had been so focused on Alastair he had taken his attention off his immediate surroundings. Searing pain followed by cold numbness raced through his arm. He had been stabbed by a Buchanan, and he watched in wonder as his shield fell from his injured, helpless arm, and his body, seemingly detached, slammed against the dusty ground of Stonehaven.

## CHAPTER 5

PRESENT DAY

When Emilia woke the next morning, she was still tired, but not as exhausted as she had been when she had first arrived. The jet lag seemed to be diminishing rapidly, which she was pleased about as she was determined to follow Fiona's advice and visit Dunnottar Castle and the MacGavin/Buchanan battlefields first thing that morning. She had finally been able to shake that odd feeling Fiona had left with her last night as she relaxed under the night sky, but when she woke this morning and stared out at the gray, she couldn't help but feel that same lump return to her chest.

She didn't know what it was, but there was something strange in the air. Emilia ignored it and dressed, throwing her rain jacket into her backpack just in case. She ate a quick breakfast before the cab arrived and she quickly jogged out to the car. It only took about ten minutes to get to the site

A TIME TO LOVE

from her cottage, and Emilia asked the driver to return in a couple of hours to pick her up since her cell signal was weak this close to the ocean.

Emilia stood looking up at the ruins of the old castle, in awe of the history laid out before her. Where others may have seen a tumble of stones, she saw so much more. She saw people who had lived and breathed, fought and loved. She turned and looked at the fields beyond, peppered with small houses now. It was here, at about this time of day, that the MacGavins clashed with the Buchanan clan. She had read of their battle, of their leader, the young Dougal MacGavin, trying to prove himself. As Emilia walked through the now manicured grasses, she couldn't help but wonder if power had anything to do with it taking so long for Dougal to become Laird.

Everything in the history books pointed to an oppressive clan leadership, but following the battle, it seemed that the elders had stepped down rather quickly. The mystery to Emilia was what had caused the sudden change. The history books were rather vague and Fiona hadn't shed any light on the subject. Emilia knew Dougal had been gravely injured, but had made it back to his castle to lead his clan. After the battle here in 1545, however, information on the MacGavin clan and the history behind it just kind of faded away.

The MacGavin name was still around in today's current Scotland, but there was a large gap in the history books after that fateful day. It was stories like these that really intrigued her, and were the reason she had majored in history — to uncover the unknown. The enigmas of history made her curiosity run wild, which was something that Bryan hated. He thought it was absurd to be so baffled about events that should be long buried. He agreed it was possible to learn from history, but that the details didn't matter. He figured if the writings stopped not long after the battle, so did their legacy, but Emilia just couldn't bring herself to believe that. There had to be more to the story. If only she could find Fiona again, perhaps she could tell her more, or at least point Emilia in the direction of where to continue her research.

Emilia felt that humans had an obsession with leaving a legacy, but in today's world, that legacy was usually captured by photos on social media, or videos stored on iPhones. The written historical record no longer seems as important. But in 16th century Scotland, this battle was one of the most important parts of their clan's existence. Emilia had a hard time believing Dougal MacGavin would have won such a battle but then disappeared into history, taking his whole clan into the darkness.

Emilia walked forward through the grasses, retracing the steps she knew would have been taken that day. First, the two leaders would have met in the middle, exchanging words. These exchanges were traditional, but didn't seem to serve much of a purpose as they never resulted in any positive outcomes. Most likely Alastair, Laird of the Buchanan Clan, rebuffed Dougal MacGavin, seeing as he lacked power and Alastair had been recorded as a flagrant, prideful man.

Then, Dougal would have turned and walked back to his troops, giving them a motivational speech. The MacGavin's battle cry, throughout their recorded history, was always "Valor and Victory," a dramatic appeal to those fighting for their freedoms. It was said that the Buchanans wished to take the MacGavins' land. If they couldn't win it outright they would leave it like they did so many others, burned to the ground and useless. They wanted an empire within the Queen's rule.

From there they would have charged the warring clan, meeting in the center of the field to begin their battle. Emilia turned and ran as the warriors would have, looking down at the grass beneath her feet. Many men would have fallen, their blood spilled on this exact ground. It was told that Dougal had looked up at Alastair, gravely grieved at the dishonor of the Buchanan's distance from the battlefield.

Emilia turned and began to climb to where Alastair would have been standing, his closest men at his side. He would have stood atop the hill and watched as his men were slaughtered. He had given them the best armor, the strongest shields, and the finest swords, but the one thing he did not give them was a purpose for which they would use those tools and sacrifice their lives.

A man with a cause could be the most dangerous in the world, especially when that cause was freedom. Emilia looked up at the mountains in the distance, imagining what it was like for the Buchanan Clan to march through the cold and fog only to be immediately met by the ferocious MacGavins. They were probably tired, hungry, and without a very good spectrum of leadership, while the MacGavins had camped, ate, and joined together as a team before facing their foe, fighting for their land, their families, and their lives.

Emilia took a deep breath and shrugged on her raincoat, pulling the hood up over her head. It was dark today, a drizzle beginning, but it wasn't enough to deter her. She turned back to face the castle remains and the empty battlefield.

As she stepped forward, she froze in shock as a flash of light streaked through the air, leaving behind the head and torso of a man, seemingly floating in midair yards ahead of her. She blinked, convinced her mind was playing a trick on her. Had she been hit by lightning? She spun around wildly to see if there was anyone else in the vicinity, but for miles around her, all she could see was emptiness. Her heart began beating wildly as Emilia slowly walked forward toward the apparition and stopped when she realized the man was injured.

She circled around the floating body, figuring that she must be losing her mind. She had become so immersed in the scene in her head, her mind had taken her there. There was no way this could be real. The man's eyes were closed and his face was stained with blood. His long dark hair was streaked with mud, his cheeks peppered with a scruffy beard.

Emilia reached her hand forward to his face, trying to figure out what she was looking at. When her hand touched his skin, warmth radiated from his body. She tilted her head but as she stepped closer to the man, there was a bright flash of light and the ground shook under her feet. Her eyes closing instinctively as she leaned forward in a crouch, her hands coming to her ears to block the strange high-pitched sound emanating from around her. Then as soon as it had begun, it was over. She remained bent over with her shoulders clenched and her eyes closed, unsure of what was going on, her body shaking with shock.

As her hearing returned, she was startled by sounds of clashing metal and screaming men. She opened her eyes and gasped in astonishment as she looked around her. She was no longer at a deserted historical monument, but instead, she was standing on a battlefield while a war raged around her. Her mouth gaped open in horror as she turned round and around, watching men fight other men, their faces covered with blood, dirt, and rage. At her feet lay the man who she saw in the field, only his entire body was now present. He was dressed as the others were in traditional Scottish clothing, and Emilia just stared at him as she tried to process what was happening to and around her.

She finally turned toward the remains of Dunnottar Castle and could only stare in astonishment. Instead of the dusty rubble that she had seen upon her arrival, standing in front of her was a castle that looked only as she had seen in movies, flames of torches lit at its walkways, movement coming from within. She shook her head in an attempt to clear it, not understanding what was happening to her as men groaned and fought around her. She had no idea what was going on but as she looked at the fallen man's crest, she recognized the symbol of the MacGavin clan.

"No," she whispered to herself, wondering who could have staged such a cruel joke. "This can't be."

Quickly she turned to face the mountains and stared up at a tall man surrounded by his closest advisors. Next to him were large thick flagpoles seeded into the ground. The crest on the flags were that of the Buchanan Clan. How was any of this possible? Emilia turned in circles watching as the same battle she just imagined played out right in front of her eyes. Only this was no stage.

She took a step forward and tripped over a body on the ground. She fell forward into the dirt and picked her hands up, holding them out in front of her face. They were covered in blood and immediately she began to panic, her breath coming in short gasps. She looked up around her as these men, these warriors who seemed so real, enacted the famous battle of the MacGavins and the Buchanans. But it couldn't be a reenactment. She would have seen them coming. Had she passed out at the time of the noise and the flash of light? But she had seen the man before that, and there had been no one else in sight when the man's body appeared floating in the air.

Suddenly she realized something. She turned her head and looked up, watching the man at the top of the hill. If that was Alastair, and these men were the warring clans, then the man on the ground could be Dougal MacGavin. She was sitting in the bloody grass watching the last moments of the battle.

She inwardly cringed — what was she thinking? There was no way this was real. There must be some explanation. Had she been struck by lightning? Was that the noise and the light that had appeared? Was this some sort of dream, or a twisted heaven for her? But how did everything seem so real? She could smell the blood and sweat of the men around her. She could feel the cold dewy ground underneath of her. She could even taste the salt in the air from the ocean. She pulled her knees to her chest as tears of panic and frustration began to fill her eyes.

She was confused and scared and had no idea what to do. She didn't even know how to extract herself to the sidelines of this battlefield without becoming caught up in the melee. So, instead of making a move, she curled up in a ball next to the wounded warrior she assumed was Dougal and watched the battle ensue, wincing every time there was bloodshed. Her head was spinning in circles and she couldn't seem to get ahold of it for even five seconds. She either needed some major medication or she had somehow been transported back to the 16th century. Either way, she had to figure out how to return to reality, and quickly, otherwise she would become a very short part of history.

"What the hell is this? Now the MacGavins bring women to their fights?" A loud voice above her shouted. "And what the hell is it that she's wearin'?"

Emilia turned toward the large bearded man and shook her head, wanting to say something but too afraid to open her mouth, completely unsure what she would even say if she did. The man laughed to himself and took a menacing step toward her. Emilia had inched forward while watching the fight and now scrambled back toward Dougal, realizing she had no way out.

How ironic, that she was to die on this battlefield. She had romanticized it in her mind, but now that she was here, she realized this battle was nothing more than death. The clansman's eyes grew dark and he raised his sword high over his head. Emilia lifted her arms up over her face in a futile attempt to shield herself and screamed out as the sword came plummeting down toward her.

## CHAPTER 6

1545

Dougal could feel himself returning to consciousness, the throbbing in his shoulder screaming at him. He groaned, grasping onto the wet grass beneath him, feeling for his sword. He forced his eyes open and blinked several times to focus them, determined not to die on this battlefield. As the blurriness disappeared, he thought he must have been imagining things as he saw a woman screaming, scrambling back toward him. What was a woman – dressed in such strange clothing – doing in the middle of the battlefield? Overtop of her was a tall Buchanan, his sword high above his head, ready to strike.

Without thinking, Dougal grabbed his sword, ignoring the pain that jolted through his body as he jumped to his feet and in one swift motion, plunged his blade deep into the chest of the Buchanan, then pulled it out as he pushed him away. Dougal watched as the body fell to the ground in a bloody heap before bringing his hand to his aching head. He must have fallen when he was stabbed and hit his head on the ground. Whoever stabbed him likely took him for dead and left him there without a final blow. That was a lucky fall, then, if it kept him from taking a sword to the heart.

Dougal sheathed his sword, seeing no additional immediate threats, and blinked again, his vision growing fuzzy once more. He took a step backward, losing his balance, as the dirt came up to meet him. The world was spinning around him so fast that he couldn't make sense of anything. All he could see was the frightened face of a woman wearing a very brightly colored strange covering. She peered down at him, looking just as confused as he felt. Maybe he was dreaming. Maybe he had hit his head so hard he was having hallucinations. As she leaned down and brushed her soft hand across his cheek, he knew she was real. She wasn't a figment of his imagination any more than the Buchanan clansmen running for the hill that Alastair no longer stood upon.

Everything in Dougal wanted to give into his body's response to sleep. His eyelids were drooping and he could feel his body trying to pull him back into an unconscious state. Everyone around him was moving in slow motion as he tried to pick his head up off the ground.

The woman he had just saved leaned over him, saying something, but he couldn't hear anything. She yelled over at someone else out of his range of vision but his head wouldn't respond to his command to turn to look. The crowd had started to gather around him as the Buchanans retreated, losing the battle without pause.

Suddenly Dougal felt hands beneath his shoulders and feet as his body was lifted from the bloody spot where he had been lying.

Once he was in the fresh grass, the woman went to work, pulling the fabric away from the top of his body, using fresh material to sop up the warm blood he could feel running down his arm and over his chest. Ivor leaned over his face and looked down at him, bringing all the noise and sounds rushing back at once.

"Ye all right?" he asked worriedly.

Dougal realized if he looked anything like what he felt, he didn't blame his friend for his concern.

Dougal nodded his head slightly, wincing as he did so, and reached up, grabbing Ivor's arm. Dougal tried to pull himself up but Ivor pushed him back down, shaking his head. He looked up past Dougal at something, then back down at him again as the woman pressed a wad of cloth against his shoulder, causing ribbons of pain to shoot through his body. Dougal gritted his teeth and growled at the pain, trying not to close his eyes in fear that he wouldn't be able to open them again.

"They retreated," Ivor said with a smile. "You did a damn good job, Laird."

Laird. He enjoyed being addressed in that way. Now all he had to do was survive to maintain the title. Dougal needed them to transport him home so that he could recover.

There was much to be done and he needed to ensure the property was well protected as Alistair would be seeking retribution following his brutal loss.

Dougal's attention shifted then, to the woman who had so mysteriously appeared by his side in the middle of the bloody battle. Even in his current fuzzy state, he realized how stunning she was. Hazel eyes were downcast, looking at his wounds, over a nose peppered with freckles, her soft face framed by flowing red hair that reminded him of fire. As his eyes traveled from her face to her body, he could only blink in astonishment at her garments.

She wore a jacket in an unnatural color of the sun, made of a strange material that the water did not touch. It hung open, and he could see beneath she wore a shirt of flowing material with some sort of picture sewn on the front of it. And on the bottom, she was wearing long underwear and exquisitely made boots of a strange leather. He wondered where she had come across such a costume and why she was wearing it. That, however, was not the most pressing question. How did she get here and why was she with his group of men?

Dougal reached out and grabbed her arm, stopping her for a moment. She looked up at him with her remarkable eyes that he now saw were flecked with gold, and he could feel a knot forming in his stomach. She was the most beautiful woman he had ever seen, despite the blood — his blood, most likely — that streaked her face. She patted his hand and smiled comfortingly as she wiped the deep scratches on his legs.

She then shook her head as she pulled the sopping cloth from his shoulder, looking at the wound underneath before replacing it. She suddenly ripped the material of her shirt, exposing her belly. Dougal tried to avert his gaze, as a woman did not show skin like that, even in the midst of battle, but her soft curves and strong build were sensual, and he felt a pull to her stronger than he had before. His thoughts, however, were interrupted as she took the ribbon from her clothing and tied it around the cloth on his shoulder, applying pressure, but with it, extreme amounts of pain. He cringed, trying not to let it show.

"I'm sorry," she whispered. "I need to stop the bleeding."

"Thank you," he said back, clasping her hand. They stared at each other for a few moments before Ivor came back into view, grabbing Dougal's legs while another man lifted him from under the arms.

"Time to go lass," Ivor said, seeming as perplexed as Dougal at the woman's presence. Dougal winced when someone brushed against his injury and placed him on a cloth gurney before hoisting him into the air.

He looked up at the gray sky as small droplets of rain hit his face, washing away the dirt and blood from his cheeks. They carried him gently but moved quickly to the camp, where they put him in the back of a wagon bed, helping the woman onto the back with him before it began to move, likely toward his home of Heatherbrook Castle.

"Yer name?" he said with a strained voice, staring up at the woman as they moved along the bumpy pass.

"Emilia," she said, looking around as if she had never seen Scotland before.

Her presence and strangeness raised more questions than they answered, but Dougal put that aside as she tended to him with as much care for him as one would a child. Several times he opened his mouth to tell her to stop, that he was a grown man who would look soft with such care, but he couldn't bring himself to refuse her touch. They rode along in silence, her hand placed firmly on his chest. Dougal could feel her soft skin against his warm body and he could not help but immediately feel a swift possessiveness over the woman, a ridiculous notion when he had no idea who she was or where she had come from, but she seemed to have attached herself to him. He couldn't say the thought upset him.

He had so many questions for her, but he knew they would have to wait until a time when he could actually form words. He knew the gravity of his injuries, had seen the steady flow of blood from the wounds. When they reached the castle she was helped down by Ivor, who then turned and picked Dougal up in his giant arms, running him into the house. Dougal could see his sister, Arabel, standing to the side with fear in her eyes as he was rushed into the great room and laid on the hard table.

"He was stabbed in the back and it looks to have gone straight through the shoulder," Ivor explained. "If it weren't fer the woman here, he'd be dead by now from the bleeding."

The clan's healing woman, Morag, had been summoned to the castle in advance of their arrival, anticipating injuries to come. When she lifted the cloths from Dougal's shoulder, he could feel fresh warm blood spilling out underneath him and gritted his teeth while she poked and prodded. When she was done examining, she nodded her head up and down and looked to Emilia.

"I'll need your assistance," said Morag, as Arabel was busy preparing hot water and cloths. Emilia nodded her head, yes, her expression confused yet determined.

"I'm going to give you some tincture," Morag said to Dougal now, her eyes soft in her wrinkled face as she looked down at him. "'Tis going to put you to sleep. Keep from fighting it. You dinna want to be awake for this."

Dougal nodded his head and couldn't stop staring at Emilia as Morag mixed some powders in water and turned back to him. Emilia helped lift him up to a sitting position, supporting his arm at the elbow to keep the pressure off his shoulder. Morag put the liquid up to his lips.

At first, it didn't want to go down, the bitter taste disagreeing with all of Dougal's senses, but as a calm started rushing over him, his throat relaxed, and he opened up and drank the cup of it. Instantly, his tense body began to ease, and he laid his head down on a wad of linen Emilia had placed underneath it. He kept watching her as the tincture began to take effect, her kind face and warm yet worried eyes his last vision as he drifted off to sleep.

In his dreams, Dougal was back on the battlefield. But there was no battle, only bodies. He looked over in the stiff breeze and saw Emilia standing there, dressed in the colors of his clan with his sister. He turned and walked over to them, looking down at Arabel's face and then up at Emilia's. She was different from when he was awake, but he couldn't quite put his finger on the change. As Arabel ran off laughing, Emilia reached out and gently took his hand, walking along the battlefield with him as if it were natural. He looked down at their hands and realized they were wearing matching rings and hand fasting ties.

There was a feeling of elation and possessiveness surging through him as he gazed at his beautiful bride. He looked up to find the elders standing in front of them, nodding in approval. They climbed the hill and looked back at the castle on the cliffs, turning toward each other and embracing. As he leaned in to kiss her lips, however, she disappeared from his grasp with a flash of light. He looked all around him but she was gone, and where bodies once laid was nothing but darkness. The smell of rotting flesh filled his nostrils as he began to run forward, looking for his bride and his home. Racing through the darkness, he couldn't see where his feet were stepping, until suddenly the light returned in a flash, and he stopped suddenly as he almost ran right off the cliffs.

Dougal turned around and faced Alastair, who was standing behind him laughing hysterically. Dougal gritted his teeth and reached for him, losing his balance and teetering on the edge of the cliff. Alastair looked over the edge and then back at Dougal before smiling evilly and pressing his finger into Dougal's wound, sending him spiraling backward toward the rocky shores below. Just before he hit the ground in his dream, he woke up sweating and breathing heavily. Arabel rushed to his side and wiped his skin with a wet rag.

"Shhh," said Morag, standing on the other side of him, checking his wounds. "You need rest. Donna waste breath on words. We seemed to be successful in repairing your shoulder but you dinna want to go and make it any worse than you already have. You did well today, son. Now you need to get better so you continue that path of goodness."

"The woman," he grunted.

"She's been escorted to a chamber," Morag said smiling. "She saved your life. Strange girl, dinna talk much at all, but she knew how to heal ye better than any other I've met in my time. Be thankful that she was there."

Thankful wasn't the only thing Dougal felt toward her. He needed to know more of this strange woman who appeared out of thin air and stepped into his life.

## CHAPTER 7

After Dougal had slipped into unconsciousness and everything had stilled for a moment as Morag went to work, Emilia's thoughts had come rushing. What was going on? Where was she? Or, better question, *when* was she? Everything had happened so quickly that she had responded without much thought, allowing her body to go into action. She had known that if she had truly been standing next to Dougal MacGavin, then it was important that he live. Everyone had looked at her strangely as she tended to his wounds but no one said anything on account that what she was doing seemed to be working quite well.

Dougal had been stabbed through the shoulder, and though she knew no major organs could have been hit, in times like these there weren't broad spectrum antibiotics or sutures that worked instantly. There were no bags of fluid or IV medications or blood transfusion capabilities, but Morag did seem to understand exactly what kind of tincture to give to him. When he was passed out and they had cleaned him and stitched him up, Emilia had stood, out of place, not knowing where to go or what to do, although she had taken a moment to clean the tools in the fire before she had given them to the healer. The woman had looked at her strangely, but had shrugged before going to work – which was when the gravity of the situation hit Emilia like a ton of bricks.

Time travel was a well-studied phenomenon, deemed impossible. Yet here she was. She knew the history well enough to realize everything she was experiencing was accurate to the 16th century, but her mind couldn't have created this world. It was too real, and contained so many unknowns that had come to life to imagine them herself. Everything was so vivid — the smells, the sights, the feel of the table and Dougal's warm skin beneath her fingertips.

"Evenin'," a young voice said behind her, startling her out of her musings. "I'm Diarmid, Dougal's cousin. I suppose you would be needing to get some rest. He should be fine tonight, as we'll be keeping a good eye on him. Follow me, I'll show ye to a room for the night. I've brought you a shirt to wear since yers seems to be torn."

"Oh," Emilia said, looking down at her bare midriff and realizing how crazed she must look to everyone in a bright yellow jacket and torn Rolling Stones T-shirt. "Thank you."

Without knowing what else she could possibly do at that moment, she silently followed the tall thin boy up the stairs and through the cavernous halls. Heatherbrook Castle, as she had heard it referred to, was a tower house, and looked to have been built fairly recently, by medieval times. It was a tall, strong building, well fortressed against potential enemies. She had read about it, but as far as she knew, it wasn't still standing today – well, today as she knew it.

Emilia tried to keep up to Diarmid while still looking around her in fascination. When he stopped in front of a door and gestured inside, she smiled her thanks as he nodded his head and walked away. Emilia shut the door behind her and looked around the room. It was simple but comfortable and she could tell it had a woman's touch at some point. The furniture was handmade from dark oak and the covering over the bed was a large grey fur blanket.

She pulled the white knit men's shirt from the bedpost and took off her rain jacket and torn T-shirt. She pulled the shirt on and tied the top, glancing over at her reflection in the window. She looked like a pirate and she wondered why these people hadn't yet thrown her out onto their doorstep. She supposed it was because of her care for Dougal. They were likely waiting for him to offer his opinion on her presence here.

Since he wouldn't be issuing orders anytime today, Emilia decided to succumb to the utter exhaustion that weighed upon her. She was just about to climb into the bed when a knock sounded on the door. She slowly opened it and peered out, finding the large man from the battlefield towering over her in a hesitant stance from outside of the door.

"Sorry to disturb you," he said bowing his head. "I just wanted to thank ye for helping out back there. Morag says Dougal surely would have been lost if it had not been for you. I'm not sure how ye got there or what yer doing in these parts, but for now, yer a savior. If you be needing anything, I'll be covering watch over Dougal where ye left him."

"Thank you," Emilia said quietly, looking up at the giant of a man. "Your name?"

"Aye. Ivor of the MacGavin Clan," he said proudly.

Emilia smiled and nodded, and as he turned away, she closed the door behind him. He had said Ivor of the MacGavin Clan like there was nothing strange about that at all. While castles of her own time's standard were still large and drafty, they were all wired with electricity and heated with alternate sources besides fires in the hearths. She saw no sign of anything modern in this place except her own clothing. As impossible as it seemed, Emilia was becoming

A TIME TO LOVE

more and more convinced of her current place in time, causing panic to flutter in her chest.

She stopped in sudden realization. Surely the man couldn't be Ivor the Terrible from the history books. Legend stated that Ivor was a key factor of the MacGavins' strength through this time of frequent clan clashes. His fierce ideas and ruthless tactics gave him the nickname, but in reality, he protected the clan many times over. It was said that he eventually died in a battle later in life. He would never give up his sword. What a strange feeling all of this was. She was living a history already written, knowing part of the ending to the story.

Emilia turned back and climbed into bed, blowing out the candles on the stand next to her. She stared up at the dark ceiling, her mind racing as she yearned to know more of what was happening, but exhaustion soon overcame everything else. Part of her hoped when she woke it would all have been a bad dream, but her ever-inquisitive mind also wanted to know more of what was happening to her, and collect more details before she determined how to find her way home. Despite the absurdity of her situation, she quickly fell into a dreamless sleep, not waking until the sun shone through the windows the next morning.

When Emilia woke, she pulled her hair back in a low ponytail, fastening it with the band she wore around her wrist. Keeping on the shirt she had been given and the leggings from her own time, she straightened herself as best she could, wishing she had a toothbrush in her bag, before she walked toward the door, half expecting it to be locked. If she were in their position, she would likely have locked her in the room, but to her surprise, the door opened up and her nose was filled with the smell of food while the laughter of children playing down the hallway reached her ears.

When she stepped out and looked around, the children

stopped their play to stare at her. The oldest of the girls, a teenager although Emilia couldn't quite place her age, stepped forward and cleared her throat. She had been assisting the healing woman yesterday, and looked quite a bit like Dougal.

"Mornin'," she said with a nod. "Me brother Dougal would be in the study. He is waiting to thank you for all ye did."

Emilia nodded and smiled, looking down the hall at the several doorways that peppered the walk. In her time, such a building would be under debate as to whether it could truly be classified as a castle. These types of structures were commonly built in the 14th and 15th centuries, designed to command and defend with limited forces. It was also typically the home of the clan leader. While it was simple, it was apparent that the important people of the clan either lived or gathered here.

Emilia carefully stepped down the creaky hallway, finally finding an open doorway with life inside. Dougal was standing in front of a shelf of books, his arm completely bandaged but his body and hair cleaned up. He was taller than Emilia had expected, standing about six feet with wide shoulders and defined muscles on display. Emilia noted the period correct kilt he wore with sashes across his bare chest in the blue and green colors of his clan. His boots rose halfway up his calf and warm fur protruded from the tops.

Her review of his clothing abruptly ended when her eyes couldn't help but linger on the hard planes of muscle underneath the sashes, and the tan of his skin beneath the dark chestnut of his hair. He was the Highlander she had long studied come to life, and a surge of desire unlike anything she had ever felt for a man of her own time – Bryan included – rose in her as she studied him.

She tentatively entered the room and stood, waiting for him to notice her.

"Yer awake," he said in a gruff tone, not raising his eyes from the ledger he was studying. "Did my family take care of ye last night?"

"Yes," said quietly. "They were very nice."

"Well, thank you for all ye did," he said, finally looking up, his smile seemingly forced. "I was told I wouldna have made it if ye hadn't a been there."

"You're welcome," Emilia replied with a smile, which quickly faded as she realized how pale his face was, dark circles under his eyes. "If you'll forgive me for saying so, you really should be in bed. Your shoulder needs time to heal and it will be difficult to tell for some time if you have suffered any long-term effects from your head injury. You've also lost a great deal of blood. Perhaps you should rest for a time?"

"Rest?" he raised thick eyebrows. "I am not sure if you are aware, lass, as you dinna seem to be from around these parts, but I am the laird of this clan. I have no time to lie in my bed 'resting,' while my people recover from the battle and make preparations around me."

"Preparations? For what?"

"War, siege, retribution — whatever the bastard Buchanan has planned for us."

"You won't do your people much good if you die," she said matter-of-factly.

"There is one thing I can assure you, lass, 'tis that I am not dying today," he said, throwing a subtle grin her way as his eyes flicked up and down over her clothing, a peculiar combination by any time's standard. "Now, we must return you to your clan. Where would they be?"

"I think that question may be difficult to answer," she replied slowly, walking forward. "I don't know if *where* is the correct question."

"I dinna understand," he said, wrinkling his nose as he looked at her impatiently.

"I… you see I…" How was she supposed to explain time travel, which she didn't really understand, to a Highlander from the 1500s? She could barely come to terms with it herself, and she had hundreds of book and movie storylines to draw from.

He stared at her with an eyebrow raised as he waited for her response.

"I am Scottish. And Irish."

He did not seem impressed with that bit of information.

"But the thing is, I'm not actually from either country. I'm from… another land. I was visiting at Dunnottar Castle, looking out at the fields. And then… well," she stumbled over her words, her eyes downcast as she couldn't meet his gaze.

"I think I may have traveled back through time," she finally blurted in a rush. "You see I'm actually from the 21st century, a historian in fact, and I was looking out at the fields remembering your battle. I don't know what happened but suddenly there was a flash of light and there you were, floating in midair. When I approached you and touched your skin, I was transported to your battlefield."

She finally looked up and met his eyes. He was staring at her incredulously, the ledger now closed, his hands fisted on the table in front of him. She could tell he was trying not to show any weakness, but it was obvious he needed the table to help hold himself up. She now knew better than to mention it, although she stayed close in case he lost his footing.

"Do you believe me to be mad?" he finally asked.

"No," she said, shaking her head. "Of course not."

"Then dinna fill my ears with this nonsense. I have no time for it," he replied, ire in his gaze.

"You think it's strange for you? Try putting yourself in my shoes," Emilia replied gruffly, without thinking of what she was saying.

"I dinna think they would fit me," he said, looking down at her boots.

Emilia held back a laugh. Of course, he had never heard such an expression.

"I dinna have the time to care for a mad woman," he continued. "I will return you to yer people if you tell me where they are, and they will surely know what to do with you."

"I'm not crazy," she said in frustration, stepping forward. "I-I'm not sure how to prove it to you. Perhaps I can tell you some of the things I know of your time, details that I could only know about if I am from the future?"

"Fine then," he said with a wave of his hand as though he just wanted to get this conversation over with. "What happens to my clan? How long am I Laird? Who leads after me?"

"Actually, that is an interesting question," she began slowly. "For there is not much recorded of the MacGavin clan past your battle at Castle Dunnottar against the Buchanans."

"That response is supposed to convince me of your claim?" he asked, looking at her with raised eyebrows.

"I can tell you about the battle," she attempted. "That was recorded fairly well."

She proceeded to describe the details of the battle, but he wasn't convinced. She could have asked any of those who had been present.

She was mid-sentence when she took a closer look at him. He seemed to be slowly sinking into the table, and his eyelids were becoming shuttered, now half closed, despite his futile attempts to stay upright and awake.

"Dougal? Er — Laird MacGavin?" She tried to meet his gaze, but his head bobbed once, twice, and she just managed to reach him when he collapsed over the table.

## CHAPTER 8

⁂

Light streamed in the window and filtered through Dougal's eyelids. As he forced them open, the pain in his temples exploded, reaching into the farthest corners of his mind and he swiftly closed his eyes once again.

Dougal winced and cursed hard. He had felt much pain before, but this was something different.

Cool fingers touched his forehead, which he welcomed as a blessing. They were replaced with an equally cold, wet cloth that somewhat eased the pain.

"Block the light, please," he heard from a low, sultry voice. As the pain in his head reduced to a dull throbbing, events from the past few days came rushing back to him. The battle, the wound, and the woman. He could tell the light had dimmed around him, and so opened his eyes to the darkened room and the beauty of the woman who hovered over him, her hazel eyes stormy with concern.

"What the devil is wrong with my head?" he ground out at her. "And why are you still here? Where is Morag?"

Ivor appeared from the corner of the room.

"The woman was with you in the study when ye fell," he

A TIME TO LOVE

said. "Arabel summoned me to come move ye to yer bedroom. She didna want the rest of the clan to know the state you were in, smart girl. Morag's with Bridget, wife of Osgar, for her babe is coming."

Dougal tried to process this through his fuzzy mind. He agreed with Ivor and Arabel — it would not do for the clan to know that their new laird was in bed after succumbing to such a weakness. He was ashamed of himself, and wished the woman had not seen him in that moment.

"If I may?" he heard the woman's voice again from somewhere in his peripheral. What was her name again? He wracked his aching brain as she eased herself beside him on the bed, holding a candle before her. The flame flickered off the planes of her face, and he was mesmerized by the glow of it. He couldn't help his suspicions of her and her mad stories, but she certainly was beautiful.

She began to move the candle toward his face, and he flinched backward, jarring his head. "What the devil—?"

"My apologies, but I would like to see if my suspicions are correct," she said softly. "Hold still if you would, and while it may be uncomfortable, if you could keep your eyes open, I'd appreciate it."

He looked at her with wariness, but didn't see any harm to doing what she asked, and so kept his gaze locked on hers as she leaned over him. She moved the light in and out of his face before shaking her head as she nibbled on her lower lip.

"I believe you have what I would term a concussion," she said.

"A what?"

"A concussion is what we call it, although I'm not a medical doctor so I cannot say for certain. You may have heard it referred to as a 'shaking of the brain.' While most physicians in this time do not understand the cause, it is from a physical jarring, which likely occurred when you fell and hit your head. Your brain moved, smashing against your skull. It can take many different forms of varying degrees of severity. When I move the light in front of your eyes, your pupils do not dilate — they don't change size, as they should with the light."

She moved her fingers around the back of his head, coming to rest on a bump high on the left side. He grimaced as even her light touch shot lightning bolts of pain through his head. "Here, this is the spot."

"How do you rid him of this?" asked Ivor, stepping up toward them.

"By summoning the physician, that is how," Dougal growled. "There is one that lives not far from here. We do not know this woman! How do we know what she says is the truth?"

"Had she wanted you dead, Dougal, she had ample time to kill you," answered Ivor with a shrug and Dougal sighed as it seemed the big man was enamored with her. "She seems to know what she's about."

"How do you know these things?" Dougal asked, turning steely eyes back on her.

"Most of what I know of medical practice is from a course I took that provided knowledge on how to help others with minor ailments – we call it First Aid," she said. "It's not extensive knowledge, but should I arrive on the scene before someone with more knowledge arrives — such as what happened on the battlefield — I can hopefully help keep someone alive and stable."

He wondered why someone would train a mad woman for such a cause. He supposed it was rational, though seldom practiced. There were many times a person would become ill or injured without a healer nearby to help. Whatever clan she hailed from had done well in determining this idea, and he resolved it would be a practice he'd begin with his own people, although not until she had returned to where she came. He wouldn't give her the satisfaction of knowing he admired the thought.

"As for causes and treatments of this time," she continued, "I taught a class on Highland Medieval medical practices. If you summon the physician, he may treat you in ways that will only serve to worsen your ailments, if not kill you."

"You, woman, are too free in your opinions and 'suggestions,'" Dougal said. He didn't like that this woman seemed to feel free to give him orders, particularly when members of his clan were present. "Summon the physician," he said to Ivor.

"I really think that—" the woman cut in.

"Summon. The. Physician."

Dougal chose not to acknowledge the laughter Ivor was holding in as Emilia rolled her eyes and sighed, moving to a chair in the corner to await the physician's arrival.

After Ivor left to fetch him, the pain in Dougal's head returned with an insistent pounding. He wanted to ask the woman to refresh the cloth on his forehead, but didn't want to admit he enjoyed her treatment. Instead, he asked her more about herself.

"Are you wed? Do you have children?" he asked abruptly, realizing he was more interested than he should be in her answer. The woman was either mad or sent by a clan to learn more of their secrets, and it would not do to have any type of feeling toward her.

"I do not have children, and no, I am not wed," she responded softly. He breathed out the air he had been holding in.

"You are not promised to anyone?"

"No," she said, and then hesitated as she seemed to be deciding whether to say more. "I suppose I had an understanding with a man for some time, but I believe we were better friends than we were anything else."

He nodded. "I see."

"From what I know, you are not wed, but are you promised to be?" she asked, those steady hazel eyes lifting to meet his.

"No, although the elders would like to see a lady of the house," he responded, closing his eyes for a moment, welcoming the solace of darkness. "But I have neither the time nor the patience to find a woman."

"No, I don't suppose patience would be an attribute of yours," she said with a bit of a smile.

"The woman is the one who needs patience," he replied.

"That is not so!" she argued. "For a strong relationship, both must trust in the other and have kindness and understanding between them."

"Then the man would not be yer husband but yer friend," he said gruffly, trying not to grimace as a wave of nausea rushed through him.

"I suppose you are — you're looking quite ill again. How do you feel?"

"Feels as if I ate bad meat," he said, suddenly feeling as if he might be sick.

He let her aid him to the side of the bed, and the moment she pulled out the pot from beneath the mattress, he heaved out his stomach contents into it. He felt rather like a child as she soothed a hand down his back. It had been some time since anyone had provided him any sort of affection. There were those he loved, including his sister, but he was the one to provide for her and offer protection, not the other way around.

Dougal felt tired again, and could feel perspiration breaking out along his body. He felt Emilia — ah, yes, that was her name

— slip the sashes off his shoulders, leaving him dressed only in his kilt. The cool air felt good against his skin, and he opened his eyes to look at her. Her gaze was on his well-defined chest muscles, but when she sensed him looking at her, her eyes flicked to the side before returning to meet his. He must have been delirious to sense any sort of desire in her glance, as the face that now looked at him was filled with concern.

"When the physician arrives," she said to him, "you must not allow him to do any sort of trepanning."

"What is this word?" he asked warily.

"Trepanning, although I suppose you might not call it such. It's a common practice for brain injury in these times. It involves driving a hole into your head to relieve whatever seems to be ailing you. There are times when this is required, such as when blood is pooling in an area of the brain, but without a sterile environment and with the equipment of this age, it results more often in death than anything else. If I'm right — and I truly believe I am — it will not help your cause at all."

He looked at her, torn between wanting to believe her and yet hung up on his own pride, not wanting to listen to the advice of a foreign woman. Drilling a hole into his head, however, was not a practice he was keen on trying.

Before he could determine the best way to agree with her without admitting it, there was a knock at the door and the physician arrived, concern on his face. Dougal lifted his arm to wave him into the room.

"My head feels as if it is splitting in two," he told him. "The woman says my brain shook against my skull when I fell and that is what is causing it. What do you suggest?

The physician didn't respond immediately, but took his time examining Dougal, looking into one eye and the other, checking his ears, his nose, and his back and chest.

"Are you going to check his eyes with the light?" asked Ivor, who had returned to stand in the corner.

The physician looked at him in confusion. "I am unsure what you mean by that."

"'Tis what the woman did," Ivor responded.

The physician took a closer look at Emilia.

"Who might you be?" he said, staring at her long and hard, whether it was due to appreciation for her looks or a suspicion in her methods, Dougal couldn't tell. "What type of healer are you?"

"She has studied common ailments and their treatments," provided Ivor, apparently now infused with admiration for Emilia who hesitated before answering his question.

"Yes, that is true," she said. "I have had the ability to learn much about the practices and treatments of conditions, many of which are not commonly practiced but are effective."

The physician nodded but seemed unconvinced.

"Well, I believe there is something inside the brain that is causing the pain," he said. "I shall return with my tools and we will free it."

"You mean boring a hole into my head?" Dougal asked.

"Well, yes, essentially," the physician responded, his eyes lifting in surprise.

"What do you suggest for treatment?" Dougal forced himself to ask Emilia.

"There is not much to do to treat this type of condition besides rest," she said, shrugging her shoulders.

Dougal looked from one to the other. He hated inaction and the thought of lying here in bed while the rest of his clan prepared for retribution from the Buchanans was unconscionable. However, the idea of a physician drilling through his skull was equally unappealing and would likely keep him from his duties for much longer.

"We shall wait," he said, seeing dismay enter the physician's eyes. "For now. Should action be required, we will take it."

Ivor saw the physician to the door then returned to Dougal.

"Is there anything else you need at the moment?"

"Nothing as of now," he said and then pointed at Emilia. "Find her some appropriate clothing. I shall rejoin you in the fields tomorrow to help with battle preparations."

"I hardly think—" Emilia began.

He quelled her protest with a long, hard stare. She gave him one of equal measure before turning and following Ivor out of the room. As she left, Dougal couldn't help but follow the movement of her shapely legs in the long underwear, as beneath his blanket his body betrayed him by reacting in desire for her.

He cursed. Whatever was he to do with this woman?

## CHAPTER 9

*E*milia followed Ivor to Arabel's room, who he said would find her more appropriate clothing to wear.

"What the devil is it that you are garbed in?" he asked her.

She stared at his back, incredulous that she was discussing her wardrobe with Ivor the Terrible. "It's called activewear. I suppose it's like a uniform of sorts. You wear certain armor for battle. I wear this clothing when undertaking activities of my own."

He turned his head to look at her, puzzled but clearly not inclined to ask her any more questions about clothing.

He knocked on Arabel's door. She swung it open, smiling at Emilia with green eyes that matched Dougal's.

"I suppose you have come for some clothing?" she asked.

"Yes, my attire is not altogether appropriate," Emilia responded.

"Come in, I ken I have a dress that you may wear. Thank you, Ivor," she said, dismissing him. Ivor sent the two women a wink before carrying on down the hallway, whistling a tune.

"He's certainly not what I imagined him to be," said Emilia.

"Ye have heard of him then?" asked Arabel. "I suppose most know the tales of Ivor and his fame in battle. 'Tis true he is a terror in warfare, but he keeps his might on the battlefield. He's rather a charming sort when there are women about."

Arabel led Emilia to the chest in the corner of the room.

"I have a dress that would suit you," she said. "You are a rather slim one, aren't you, though you are a touch taller than I am. We may need a bit of stitching to hold it up on you, but otherwise it should be fine."

Arabel concentrated on the material as she had Emilia try on the dress. She pinned it and sewed it until she was satisfied. Her fingers were deft and skilled, and Emilia was impressed by her aptitude with the needle and thread.

"There now," she said when finished, clasping her hands together in front of her. "You look quite fetching in the MacGavin blue. We shall wash your other garments and you can keep them for... for when you like."

Emilia appreciated the kindness of Dougal's sister and her willingness to accept her and not ask questions about where she came from and why she was dressed this way. She wondered at the difference in the siblings and their attitudes. She supposed it had all to do with the roles of male and female in this time, and Dougal's concerns in his role of leader.

She looked at herself in the smoky mirror in the corner. She had to admit she agreed with Arabel's assessment. From what she could see, the color did suit her. She followed Arabel down the hall and back toward the kitchens. Arabel showed her where they did the washing and the cooking. She didn't explicitly ask Emilia to help with any of the chores, although she insinuated that should Emilia be staying with them for some time, perhaps she wouldn't mind helping with the odd task. Emilia was more than happy to agree in order to keep from idleness, and Arabel sent her into the yard to gather beans and peas for the dinner.

Emilia was picking the best of the bunch and placing them into the bag she had brought from the kitchens as she pondered how long she truly would be here in this time, when she heard voices to her left. It was two of the clansmen, she assumed, talking lowly to one another so she could not hear what they said. They were looking her way, but averted their gazes when she looked up to meet their stares.

She realized it was to be expected that she would be of interest to the clan. Many of the men had seen her at the battlefield, and now she was staying in the home of their laird. The sun beat down on her as she picked pea pods, and she noticed many passed by, interested in a glimpse of the mysterious woman.

When she figured she had enough, she returned inside, provided Arabel with the vegetables, and helped her chop.

"If Dougal is gruff with you, do not let it concern you," said Arabel, her voice low so none could hear. "He likes to maintain a foreboding presence, but he cares deeply for those he loves. He intimidates, but he protects. He has allowed ye to stay here, so as much as he may not show his appreciation for yer assistance, the fact yer still here means something."

Emilia nodded, contemplating what Arabel said to her. She could see the truth in Arabel's words, and understood not only the position of laird, but the role of women in this time. Arabel was a wise woman already, despite the fact she was in her teens. Emilia suddenly stopped peeling the potato. If Arabel was in her teens, how old did that make Dougal? Emilia had spent far too much time admiring his perfect body and suddenly wondered if she had desired a man far too young for her. He seemed close enough to her age, but times were different.

"Arabel," she said, trying for nonchalance. "How old is your brother?"

"He is four and twenty," Arabel said with a small smile, not fooled for a moment by Emilia's question. "Which is why the elders want him to marry. He is far too old not to take a bride, especially for a leader."

Emilia nodded. He was young, yes — but only a few years younger than she is. She breathed a sigh of relief. Her attraction, then, while nothing more than that, was not creepy at least. When the vegetables were done, she wiped her hands on a cloth and excused herself. "I best check on your brother," she said, and as Arabel nodded at her, she turned and made her way up the stairs.

She pushed open the door gently, finding Dougal fast asleep in bed. She had reached the limit of her knowledge of concussions. She didn't think there was much else that could be done to treat them, and yet she knew Dougal wouldn't be content to rest much longer.

She also knew she would have to keep a close eye on his shoulder and hope the wound wouldn't become infected. There was no telling what had entered into it along with the sword. They had done a fairly good job of cleaning it but there was certainly no such thing as antibacterial wipes or solutions – let alone a healthy use of soap – in these times.

She sat beside Dougal, staring at his face in peaceful restfulness. His stubbornness was annoying but also understandable. She wished he was a little more agreeable, but she understood he would have no reason to trust her, and that her story was completely unbelievable. She hardly believed it herself, and she was living it.

Emilia leaned over him to try to take a closer look at his shoulder wound while he slept, but when her hand reached out to lift the bandage, suddenly his large fingers engulfed her wrist, though his eyes remained closed.

"'Tis difficult for me to rest when a beautiful woman drapes her body over mine in bed," he said, his voice low in her ear.

"Laird—"

"You may call me Dougal."

"Dougal, then. I did not mean to — that is, I was just simply checking—"

"There is no need to explain yourself," he said. "I find I do not mind all that much."

He hooked his other arm around her body, bringing her down toward him. She landed on top of him with an "oomph."

"You really must be careful—"

"Shush woman," he said as she brushed against his jutting manhood and she swallowed hard at the fact that she could be causing such a reaction from him. Before she could gather her thoughts he sent her reeling with a hard kiss on her lips. She pushed her palms into his chest, at first in an attempt to push him away. But as his tongue teased her lips, she stopped thinking as her body took over. Soon instead of trying to extract herself, her nails were digging into his broad chest, as she craved more of the passion he was showing her. She had never felt anything like this before. She had been attracted to Bryan, but this — this was altogether different. This was a desire that she felt from the depths of her soul.

The man was stubborn, arrogant, and rude to her, but that didn't detract from his sexual appeal. At this moment, she appreciated the dedication to which he undertook his every task, as he showed her exactly the type of lover he would be — one who was thorough, passionate, and who took care for her own satisfaction as well.

He cupped her bottom through her dress with one hand

while his other lifted the elastic from her hair. He seemed to pause as he couldn't find the end of it to untie, but eventually slid it down her ponytail and ran his fingers through her freed crimson tresses.

She was in awe of him, physically. This was the type of man she read about, the masculine warrior who haunted her desires. She gave as good as she took, and did not stop to think of the path they were headed down until there was a knock at the door.

Emilia jumped off him, rearranging her dress as she took up a seat next to the bed and turned to face the door. Dougal simply looked at her with a carnal smile before answering with a "come in."

It was Ivor, and after a glance from one of them to the other, he seemed quite in tune with what had just occurred in this room as he gave his friend a knowing grin.

"Dougal," he said, "My sincerest apologies for interrupting. I felt ye'd want to know at once, however, that we caught a Buchanan lad within the keep. He may have been accompanied by another, but he's the only one we have found thus far. Would you like to question him, or shall I do so for ye?"

Emilia shivered as Ivor seemed thrilled at the prospect of his role as inquisitor.

"I'll come with ye," said Dougal, his countenance hard.

Before Emilia could say anything, Dougal, anticipating her resistance, silenced her with a look. He pushed himself up to a sitting position, then swung his legs over the side of the bed. He paused for a moment as if preparing himself, and then stood. He swayed for just a moment before making his way slowly along the bed.

He dressed once more in his sashes, and went to the basin in the corner to splash water onto his face.

Emilia watched him closely the entire time, nibbling on her lower lip in nervousness.

"I should like to see the man suffer myself," he said, the rage in his face making Emilia take a step back. "I must also show my clan that I am a leader they can believe in."

"As long as you don't pass out first," she finally broke in, unable to stop herself. He turned his glare onto her, but said not another word as he sheathed his sword into his waist belt, and walked out of the room with Ivor, leaving Emilia behind staring after him.

She blinked her eyes and dug the pads of her fingers into her palms. She was partially awed with his resolve. She knew it would have taken considerable strength to push himself out of bed, especially without showing any ounce of weakness. But that was who he was. A strong man, whose lack of displays of vulnerability could lead to his ultimate defeat. She noted the patch of blood staining the bed where his shoulder wound had rested. She'd meant to check underneath the dressing but had been… distracted.

She could not believe she had kissed Dougal MacGavin. What was she thinking? She must find a way to return to her own time soon, and therefore could not afford to form attachments here. Yes, she was attracted to Dougal — what woman wouldn't be? — but she could not let it get the better of her. Besides that, she reminded herself, he was rude, stubborn, and seemed to have a rather high opinion of himself. She tried not to think of his better qualities although couldn't quite help herself. She sighed. Damn the man.

## CHAPTER 10

Dougal shook his head as he stormed out of the room, leaving the woman and his inability to resist her behind him. He did not know what to make of this Emilia, who had so suddenly appeared into their midst. She was beautiful, intelligent, and strong. Yet she was also very strange, rather forward, and certainly kept her secrets. He could not trust her, not at this point, but that did not keep his desires at bay.

When he had awoken to her leaning over him, he could not keep himself from her. She had tasted as good as he had imagined, like a field of roses. He squared his shoulders as he and Ivor neared the back door. Now was not the time to be thinking of beautiful women, as desirable as this one might be.

Dougal noted Ivor kept a close eye on him as they made their way to the gatehouse where the Buchanan soldier was being held. He felt like a woman who had succumbed to a swooning spell. He was dismayed by the weakness he had shown, and had to ensure that the clan saw him as the strong leader he was. He noted that many of his people had formed a gathering around his keep, eager to learn more about the captured Buchanan. Dougal also realized that while he had led his men into battle, this was the first time his clan had seen him as their true laird.

He nodded to Ivor, a sign that he felt fine and knew what he was about, and then climbed the steps to the front entrance of his home in order to address the crowd before him.

"MacGavin brothers and sisters!" he shouted. "Today I address you as your laird. It is a privilege and an honor to do so. We are a long and storied clan, strong on the battlefield, known for our stealth and our heroism. Valor and Victory is our cry — upholding our courage through everything we face as we defeat our enemies! In our homes we treasure our family, be it blood relatives or the clan ties that hold us together. I have been raised knowing I have the full support of the McGavin clan, and I treasure each and every one of you.

"Two days ago we won a decisive victory over the Buchanans, who want to take our land and our homes from us. I know many of you lost brothers, fathers, and sons in that battle. I feel the pain of every one of you, as I lost my own father to Alastair Buchanan many years ago. We have run them off for now, but we must continue to remain strong and vigilant. I vow to spend my life protecting all of you.

"Today we begin by questioning the Buchanan that has come into our midst. I will face him myself to learn what it is he wants from us, why he's spying among us. He will not go free for his sins against us. Valor and Victory!"

As Dougal raised his fist in the air and shouted the battle cry, his clan's voices ringing with his, he looked up and saw Emilia standing at the back of the crowd. She had an unreadable expression on her face, and he realized with a curse that he *cared* what she thought, of him and his leadership. He grimaced at the thought as he looked at her, and she seemed to misinterpret his look as she walked away. Bloody women. He had no time for this, as he had told the elders.

He walked carefully down the steps and through the cheering clan. His vision was still blurred, his head still throbbed, and if he looked at the sun high in the sky, pain stabbed into his brain. But he would not let his clan see any weakness. He kept his gaze down and blinked his eyes, grateful for the reassuring Ivor close by his side.

When they had rounded the corner toward the outbuilding, Dougal paused for a second to catch his breath before continuing inside. There sat the Buchanan, bound in rope and surrounded by MacGavin men. He had a smug look on his face until he caught sight of Dougal and Ivor in the doorway. His smile fell as his head swung wildly from one side to the other as though he might be able to seek out escape.

"Buchanan," said Dougal, his voice dripping with ire. "What brings you here, to our home? Do not tell me a lie, as it will only make things worse for you."

"I took meself out for a stroll, I did, and came upon your fine home," said the Buchanan, although the satisfaction in his voice wobbled for a moment.

Dougal nodded at Ivor, who gave the man a taste of his meaty fist. As the Buchanan spit blood out of his mouth, he looked up at the giant Ivor the Terrible, and reconsidered his original position.

"Verra well, then," he said to Dougal before heaving a great sigh. "Our laird wanted to know if you were still alive. He had heard you were felled on the battlefield and wanted proof of your death. He wanted to know who was in charge of the MacGavin clan, and where you were vulnerable so we could exact revenge."

Dougal eyed him closely. "Are you alone?"

"Alone…?"

"Did ye come alone?"

The Buchanan looked from Dougal to Ivor, then at the floor as he considered his options. Ivor took a step toward him.

"Fine, fine," he said, shrinking back away from them. "I was not alone. There was another with me, but he was much faster than me and ran when we were found by yer men."

As Dougal swore under his breath, Ivor gave the man a backhand across the face for no reason other than he felt like it. Dougal asked the Buchanan if he knew what Alastair planned to do with the information, but he protested that he had no idea, that Alastair would never share that with someone like him. At the fear in the man's eyes, Dougal reluctantly had to believe him.

He told his men to lock the prisoner inside until he determined what would be best to do with him. He figured he would eventually release him, once he knew what Alastair's plans were. While Ivor would like him killed, the man had cooperated, and for that Dougal would spare his life.

As he began walking back toward the house, he commented to Ivor how warm it was. Ivor looked at him strangely out of the corner of his eye, remarking that the weather had actually cooled over the day.

"What?" Dougal asked when Ivor wouldn't stop staring at him.

"Ye dinna look so well, Dougal," he said. "Yer skin is pale and pasty, and ye look as if you may fall over in the wind."

Dougal snorted at him. "Donna be ridiculous, Ivor. I've weathered far worse pain than this. So I had a simple knock to the head, what about it?"

He returned to the castle, telling Ivor to stay and eat with the family. With his uncle and cousin joining them, dinner was focused around tales of the battle the day before. Arabel had ensured Emilia ate with them, though she sat at the end of the table with her head bowed, as if she were avoiding Dougal. Which was fine by him. The farther away from him she stayed, the better.

He explained her presence to his uncle as a traveler they had come across near the battlefield who was on her way to rejoin her clan. His uncle didn't look like he completely believed Dougal's words, but he didn't question them.

Dougal had not much of an appetite, but instead listened to Diarmid's tales. The boy had heard of the battle from the men of the clan, and was happy to tell the stories as if he had been there himself. Diarmid greatly exaggerated Dougal's heroism, wound, and subsequent recovery, but Dougal didn't mind seeing the excitement on the boy's face and, truth be told, he didn't quite have the strength to protest.

When dinner was over, Dougal made his excuses and headed to his bedchamber, exhaustion settling over his body. His shoulder ached, but when Emilia knocked on the door to look at his dressing, he turned her away.

For if she entered the room, he knew that even in his current state, he would take her, and he didn't know enough about her to trust she wasn't here for the Buchanans or another clan that wished him harm. As he drifted off to sleep, however, his mind turned on him and made his desires into his dreams.

\* \* \*

DOUGAL WOKE the next morning bathed in sweat, and not from his all-too-vivid imaginings throughout the night. When he blinked his eyes open, his vision had further blurred, and his shoulder ached furiously.

The door creaked open, and his hulking friend stepped in.

"Ivor," Dougal croaked. "Summon the physician."

The man nodded, and Dougal could read the concern on his face.

"And Ivor…" he added, "Keep quiet about this. The clan doesna need to know their laird is ailing."

"Aye," the big man agreed with a word, and walked out, shutting the door loudly behind him.

Dougal tried to push himself up from the bed, but his arm gave out and he collapsed back down on the mattress.

When he next opened his eyes, the door was opening once more, admitting Ivor, Emilia trailing behind him. But hadn't Ivor left but moments ago? How long had it been since he had gone for help?

"What is she doing here?" he mumbled, not wanting the woman to see him in his current condition.

"She seems to understand your ailment," said Ivor mumbled. "Thought she might be more help than the physician."

Dougal let out a curse under his breath, watching as Emilia walked over to him with a cool cloth. He flinched at first, but allowed her to bath his face and the rest of his body. It felt good — too good. He was annoyed at Ivor, though, for bringing her here when he had asked for the physician.

She reached for the dressing on his wound to tend to it, and once again, he was shamed that he had been felled so easily on the battlefield. As she continued to bathe his body, he realized that at least part of him had stirred to life once more, and he needed to be rid of her before she – or Ivor – saw what she was doing to him.

"If you touch me bloody shoulder again, I'll have you out of here on your arse!" he growled at her. "What part of leave me be do you not understand, woman?"

## CHAPTER 11

*E*milia took a breath, calming the angry response that threatened. Dougal was clearly ill, and while she was aware that women didn't garner the same respect they did in the 21st century, she had seen the kindness Dougal extended to his sister and knew he was capable of better.

"I will not be spoken to like that," she said, her voice level. "I believe I have proven myself to be treated with a bit more dignity."

He looked down at her, his eyes a stormy green and his tone terse. "I am Laird of the McGavin Clan, and you, lass, remain a guest in my home only because I will it to be so. I will speak to you however I may wish, and if you dinna like it, you may leave!"

"If I leave, you may die," she said, wondering how much of his outburst was the result of the pain he was hiding. "Wounds of this sort often lead to tetanus or gangrene. I imagine the sword that went through your body had gone through a few men before you. With that, followed by the gore of the battlefield, infection is likely. By not allowing me to take a look yesterday, it likely led the infection to worsen. You must let me see it now."

"Infection?" questioned Dougal, as he and Ivor looked at her in confusion.

"It's festered," she explained, realizing they would think infection meant disease.

After a few tense moments, he relented with a nod. She pulled the cloth back from the wound on his shoulder and tried not to gag at the smell emanating from it. Despite everything she had done, what Morag had done, this wound was infected, and badly. She assumed it was from the battlefield, from whatever filth had entered it with the sword and seeped in while he lay there in the dirt, knocked unconscious.

She wished she had been more insistent last night. She had tried to visit his room to replace the dressing but he had refused to allow her entrance.

She had been unsure what her next course of action would be — did she leave Dougal MacGavin and his clan as they were? He certainly didn't appreciate her help. But she also couldn't bring herself to return to her time without seeing this story through. She had become part of it, willingly or not, and this was one tale she must finish.

"Dougal, I must be honest with you — you're not in a good situation. This wound is worsening quickly. I'm not sure what else I can do for you without antibiotics."

"Without who?"

"Antibiotics. It's a medication that will be discovered in some few hundred years. It fights bacteria and infection, although now we are beginning to overuse it and at some point in time—"

She stopped when she realized she was rambling and he had no idea what she was speaking about. "Anyway, it would heal you. However much as I have studied medical knowledge of this time, I do not know what other methods that would be available to us can be used for you."

She moved in front of him, feeling his jawline and his forehead. He was warm to the touch of her fingertips and she tried to push aside the panic that filled her belly to prevent him from seeing how dire his situation was fast becoming.

"I believe fever is setting in. We can fight it with some of the herbs and poultices but unless we heal the infection in the wound…" she trailed off, biting her lip.

"I'm a dead man?"

"Few recover from this type of injury once infection sets in."

"You say few. I am a strong man, lass, and I refuse to let a scrape like this take me. I have not only survived, but led infamous battles across the Highlands. I will not die in my own bedchamber of an illness caused by the sword of a Buchanan!"

Emilia pushed her fingertips into her temples as she tried to determine her best course of action. If only she knew how she had gotten here in the first place or what her purpose here was, it would make everything a lot easier. "I believe," she said slowly, "it would be best if I do whatever I can to return to the future and see what I might be able to retrieve for you. While I'm there I will pick up some books on natural healing to see how else I can treat you in this time."

He frowned at her, mulling over her words, as he clearly still didn't believe her.

"Perhaps when I return with the medication you will be more likely to believe in what I'm telling you," she said, raising her arms helplessly to either side. "You must trust in me. Twice now, I have shown you that I mean to do you no harm but rather do all I can to save you. All I ask of you is to allow a member of your clan to show me the way back to the battlefield. I'm not sure I can find it on my own and it's the only place that might reasonably be my gateway home."

"Fine," he said sighing. "I shall take ye myself. We leave after breakfast."

"You are in no condition to leave this bed, let alone accompany me to the battlefield," she exclaimed.

"You have said many things to me since you have arrived, but not much of it has been truth," said Dougal stubbornly. "I will come with you and see where you find this witchcraft of yours. I am eager to meet yer clan and have my questions answered. Should you truly believe in this tale you have spun for me, when we arrive at the battlefield and you realize you have gone mad, we can then determine what to do with ye."

There was no arguing with this man, that was for certain. "They say you can only help those who agree to help themselves," she finally murmured to herself before addressing him again. "You best eat something before we leave. I would prefer you didn't pass out on me again. I can't lift you alone."

"I'll join you at the table."

"I think you should—"

"Enough of what you think. Need I remind you that I may do as I please and am not required to listen to the orders of others, least of all a woman, who is not even of my own clan."

Emilia turned on her heel, away from the stubborn, hostile man and made for the kitchens, leaving her simmering frustration in her wake. She hadn't been sure what her next course of action should be, and now the decision had been made for her. She would return to the future, apparently with Dougal at her side, and she could then send him back with the medication and continue with her own life.

They ate breakfast in silence as Dougal's family picked up

on his mood. She could tell his sister was questioning their journey to the battlefield, but Arabel kept her questions to herself, apparently used to Dougal's moods. After breakfast, Emilia packed her 21st century clothes and followed Dougal to the stables, where they mounted horses and took off for the fields. It was only Emilia's second time riding a horse and she noticed he watched her struggle to mount and seat herself out of the corner of his eye.

She glared at him as he snickered, considering maybe there was a reason that he didn't show up in the history books after the battle. No one liked a hero who was also a jerk.

"Are you sure you should be riding?" she asked him.

He snorted and kicked his horse into a trot, clearly expecting her to follow behind him.

She sighed. Damn the man.

As they rode, she tried to explain to him what traveling through the portal had been like for her, and what he could expect in her time. He looked at her incredulously as she spoke of motorized wagons, buildings made of metal, and storehouses full of goods. Eventually she gave up trying to prepare him and they continued on their journey in silence.

When they arrived at the battlefield, they dismounted, tied their horses, and walked out to the hill where Alastair had stood days before. All the Buchanan bodies had been removed and buried, but the grass lay stained in blood. Emilia looked out to the center of the field where she had first seen Dougal's body. Was it her imagination, or did the air look... different there? It seemed like a haze stood between her and the landscape beyond, like if she moved her hand forward, it would move through a wall of clear jelly.

She grabbed Dougal's hand and pulled him down the hill and toward the portal. He followed along with a grunt.

"Wait here," she said, before stepping into the trees to change into her leggings, torn T-shirt, and jacket.

When she returned, she noted that Dougal slightly listing to one side apparently hadn't noticed the incandescent glow of the transportation hole yet, but when she pointed him toward where she had arrived and they stopped in front of it, she heard him suck in his breath.

He was nothing if not a brave man, and he reached out to touch the shimmering air with his fingertips, his eyes widening as they disappeared through it.

"Wait here for me?" she asked, looking up at him, her heart beating fast.

"I will come with you," he said, surprising her, his gaze hard.

"Dougal—"

"I will come."

She already knew there was no arguing with him and decided there was no time like the present.

Emilia took in a deep breath and before either of them could question the decision, reached in herself, interlaced her fingers with Dougal's and stepped into the portal, pulling him along with her. Lightning flashed around them, and she kept her focus on Dougal, whose eyes widened in fright and bewilderment — emotions she sensed he very rarely felt, or if he did, ever displayed.

Suddenly it felt as if they were falling, the ground disappearing below them as they were pulled toward a bright light in the darkness that began to surround them. Emilia closed her eyes and braced herself for the fall. Then strong arms wrapped around her, and instead of hitting the ground, she hit a solid chest.

She rolled off Dougal, opening her eyes to see the cliffs as she had only a few days before — was that all it had been? — aged with time, the castle beyond them in ruins.

Dougal squatted in a battle stance as his head whipped around him, looking around wildly at his surroundings. He likely was taken off guard by the events that were quickly unfolding, as he had admittedly never believed there was any truth to what she had told him.

Emilia asked him if he was all right, but he ignored her and began circling the area, his hand on his sword as his gaze repeatedly strayed to the ruins in front of him.

"Dougal," she said again, and he opened his mouth to respond, but nothing came out.

Emilia remembered her own shock at being transported back to the battlefield, and while she knew she had prepared him, she could only imagine what he must be feeling now.

"What type of sorcery is this?" he asked, his voice low and raspy, and Emilia put herself in front of him, imploring him to believe what she was saying.

"I wish I had a better answer for you," she said, tentatively placing a hand on his good shoulder. "I was as shocked as you were when I was brought back to your time. Whatever this magic is, I didn't create it, but it seems it has availed itself to us."

"I've never much believed in sorcery, but this…" he waved his sword at everything around him. "This is unexplainable."

"I know," Emilia said softly. "Dougal, I'm not sure how much time we have. I need you to trust me here, and for once, follow my lead. Can you do that?"

He looked over at her, his mouth hooking into a little half-grin that caused something deep in her belly to respond with a curl of desire of its own.

"I suppose I have no choice."

She held a hand out toward him, question in the action, and he hesitated for just a moment before placing his large, strong hand in hers, wrapping his fingers around her palm, causing a tremble to begin from where they had joined and rush through the rest of her body.

Emilia realized she had to ignore it – for now – and instead, turned him in the direction of the ports. They would have to walk, as she knew that calling for a taxi would not be the smartest of ideas. She took a breath and did her very best to explain to Dougal what he would be facing when they reached civilization. She had no idea whether Dougal was listening to a word she said, for he said nothing, his expression a mixture of curiosity and distrust.

Of course, she understood. While Emilia had the advantage of understanding his history when she traveled back to his time, he knew nothing of what was to come in the future, nor could he ever imagine what would be awaiting him even if he had believed her. This would seem like another world entirely.

When they reached the edge of Stonehaven ports, Emilia stopped and turned toward Dougal. He looked so strong and handsome standing next to her, his eyes roaming the distance. Emilia felt that pull to him again, from both her heart and deep within the center of her being. He was honestly the most desirable man she had ever seen in person, and yet completely intimidating. She had always been more for the bookish type, not a man who would so easily and willingly dominate her. And yet… she liked it. She liked *him*. For as obstinate as he had been, she understood where it all came from, why he felt he needed to act the way he did, and the fear that was currently driving it.

His muscles rippled, his skin tan and warm. His green eyes sparkled in the sunlight. Emilia caught his arms in her hands as she stood in front of him, intent on making him actually listen to her.

"There are going to be many things here that you don't understand," she explained. "But I need you to keep it together and stay very close to me so we don't raise any eyebrows. Okay?"

"Aye," he responded simply, locking eyes with her, deep within her very soul.

Emilia began to make a checklist for herself. A pharmacy first, for sterile dressing and any medications they would give her. She would have to hope that they would give her antibiotics without a prescription. She could hardly imagine taking Dougal to see a doctor – she couldn't see it going well for Dougal nor the doctor.

As they walked down the streets, Dougal's head whipped back and forth as he looked around himself in wonder. What must electricity, motor vehicles, and buildings constructed in ways he could never envision look like to him? It was fortunate they were in Stonehaven and not New York City, but still, how drastically the world had changed in a few hundred years.

Emilia spotted the pharmacy across the street and pointed it out to Dougal, explaining why they were going there and what she would be buying.

She swiftly jogged across, pulling at Dougal's hand. Before she realized what he was doing, he had dropped her hand and she took a few steps before realizing that he wasn't with her. Immediately, the sound of horns began to blare behind her. Apparently, her explanation of vehicles hadn't been enough to make him understand anything about them. She swiveled around swiftly and watched as Dougal crouched down in the street with his sword outstretched toward the driver of a car. Emilia jogged out and grabbed him by the arm, mouthing an apology and a wave to the frightened driver. She pulled Dougal toward the shop and stopped when they had cleared the road, looking up at him.

"It's going to be all right," she said, hating the frightened look in his eyes, the eyes of a man who could stare down thousands of armed men without fear. "I won't let anyone or anything here hurt you. I know it must all seem incredibly…." She stopped, realizing that telling him she understood his fear would only put his back up all the more. "Shocking and unbelievable. We are going in here to get the medicine, and then I'll send you back. I promise. Do you trust me?"

## CHAPTER 12

The darkness of the tunnel had sent Dougal's head spinning all over again, and like his dream, he and Emilia had whirled through an unknown space heading toward a bright light at the end. He had looked down as the field grew closer once again, bracing himself when they were about to hit the ground. He had positioned his body under Emilia's to break her fall, careful not to let her see the pain in his shoulder when she had landed on top of it.

As she rolled off him, he had reached out and steadied his body, looking around at the battlefield. The grasses were short and the castle on the cliffs had fallen to disarray, with only partial walls still standing. As he prepared for possible threats to arrive, Dougal had noticed the salty sea was still in the air, but the scent of blood and battle was long gone. When he had finally looked over at Emilia, she had been dusting herself off, her lip between her teeth as she had stared at him with concern.

He would never admit it to her, but there was something about her that did make him feel grounded, no matter what was happening around them. When she had taken his hand, he was able to finally take a breath, and somehow he knew that if she was with him, they would make it through whatever strange land this was in front of them.

The roads were still there, but they now appeared more like black stone than the familiar dusty trails. Large poles protruded from the ground with thick, shiny metal ropes hanging from them, connecting from one to another as far as his eyes could see.

If this was the future, thought Dougal, perhaps he should have let Alastair have it after all. He had tried not to shudder at the loudness of the waves, nor the large, strange ships that floated at the docks. Big metal boxes stood atop them as the water churned beneath them from some unknown contraption below. Nothing of the bustling city was familiar, but seemed to be from another place entirely. This was a different world, one of unforgiving hard surfaces and noise, and he did not want any part of it. Everyone was dressed like Emilia, in bright, unseemly clothing. Lamps without fire were lit all around them, while the buildings were painted in words and designs.

He had agreed with everything Emilia had said to him without really thinking through his response, as he was too overcome by his surroundings. He had held onto her as though she was a small boat in the middle of the ocean, the only thing keeping him from drowning completely.

Had it not been for the throbbing pain in his shoulder, he would have thought to be dreaming once again, still under the influence of Morag's tincture. As it were, there was nothing feigned about what he was seeing, and he had stopped momentarily to stare at the front of a glass-walled building. Beyond the glass, large thin boxes showed him moving pictures inside. He tilted his head, wondering how those people were inside the box, and why were they so small? It seemed magic had overcome all, and they were all bewitched here, accepting of the spells in this puzzling time.

Dougal had kept quiet, all of his senses alert as he had followed Emilia, who moved him quickly through the bewildering number of people around them. They had walked along the hard stone ground and he couldn't help but wonder how they had built it so smooth. He preferred the stone walkway they had travelled when they had first entered this strange town.

Dougal had allowed Emilia to lead him to the other side of the road, but froze and dropped her hand as a large metal monster rolled through the street, screaming loudly at them. There was a human inside the monster's body, and Dougal had crouched down and drawn his sword, ready to fight this monstrous beast.

Which was when Emilia had quickly run over and grabbed his arm, shaking her head and pulling him out of the street. She didn't seem to be frightened by these monsters at all, and the human inside seemed to be perfectly fine with being there.

That's when she had asked if he trusted him.

"I…"

He didn't want to. He wanted nothing to do with this strange time and place, wished that they were back in his home, where he could still be satisfied with not believing her and her strange musings, with thinking her mad.

He didn't like that he had no choice *but* to trust her, for at the moment, she was the only familiar part of this place.

But strangely, he did trust her, and for more reason than simply the fact that she was likely the only way he could make his way out of this hell and return home. He didn't understand this willingness to trust a strange woman he had only just met, but he also couldn't help the tie he felt toward her, and found himself nodding in response.

"I do," he said simply, and relief rushed over her face, as she stepped toward him and took both of his hands within hers.

"Dougal, you do not need to be frightened of the cars, but you do need to stay out of their way," she said. "You ride a horse to get from one place to the other — well, now we have these machines for transportation. They're mechanical. If you will listen, I'll explain them to you in detail later, but I promise, they will not hurt you if you just avoid them."

What a strange way to get around. Dougal didn't see any horses whatsoever. Did they no longer exist? How did the beasts move?

"Let's do this quickly. Stay with me."

Dougal nodded and followed her into the store. Light, like sun captured in boxes, was bright and painful to his throbbing skull, but he stayed silent as she walked through the rows of an inconceivable number of goods, collecting what appeared to be bandages and bottles of what he supposed was the medicine she kept speaking about from the large shelves made of a strange, smooth material unlike anything he had ever seen before.

There were brightly colored boxes everywhere but they were not made of wood. It was some flimsy material that Dougal could not see lasting very long. He watched as she piled the items on the table at the front.

A man on the other side of the table looked at Dougal strangely as he dragged the items across a glass and metal box that let out a squeal every time he did. Dougal glowered back at him.

"My friend here needs some penicillin," Emilia said, leaning over the counter with a smile at the man. Dougal didn't like the way she looked at him, realizing with unease that he wanted those smiles directed at him and him alone, even though he knew he had done nothing to deserve them.

A TIME TO LOVE

"Do ye have a prescription?"

At least this man's voice wasn't as foreign as Emilia's was. Dougal wondered at her strange land of origin.

"We did, but we lost it," she said, her voice low and smooth as she looked at him from beneath her eyelashes. "It's just a low-dose antibiotic, nothing too strong. It was so difficult to get into the doctor to start with, I don't suppose you could do us a favor? Even a sample?"

The man in the white coat seemed conflicted, and Dougal placed a hand on his sword, ready to command him to do whatever Emilia said. Apparently sensing his intention, she reached a hand behind her and placed it over his, stilling the action, although Dougal didn't move his hand from the hilt of the weapon.

Finally, the man heaved a great sigh and leaned in toward Emilia. Dougal stepped forward to push him back and away from his woman – where had *that* come from – but Emilia blocked his way.

"Fine," the man said with a grumble. "Just a few samples. But I can't have ye telling anyone or I'm in for it."

"Of course," Emilia said, squeezing Dougal's fingers beneath hers. "Thank you so much."

Emilia pulled out something small and rectangular and gave it to the man. He quickly slid it through another metal box and handed it, with the items, back to her. She turned to Dougal and nodded, nudging him toward the door.

"Thank goodness," she said, her breath coming out in a rush. "One more quick stop," she said, leading him to the front of a stone building which was more familiar to him, though he could not understand why every building had a name attached to it, as if people did not know where they were.

They went inside, and he was astonished at the number of books lining the walls around them. This however, he thought with a rush of relief, was familiar. He knew what books were, recognized the solid wood table and chairs.

Emilia searched through the shelves and then surveyed a few of the books she had pulled out. She looked surprised by the first, then made notes of what appeared to be herbal remedies from another. He was starting to become impatient – and a fair bit dizzy and warm – when she nodded her head and stood, ready to leave.

"Alright," she said once back out on the noisy street. "I need to get you back to the portal before you get arrested or thrown in a mental institution."

"A what?"

"Nevermind." She sighed. "Come on."

They made their way back out of the port and walked to the cliffs. Each step felt heavier, although Dougal wasn't about to admit it to Emilia. Once they were back in the quiet of the fields, Dougal took a deep breath, relieved to be back on land that was familiar and away from the rush of the city, even though it still didn't look right to him.

Both of them looked down at all Emilia held within the paper bag, including the scribbled notes she had made in the library. She seemed to be deep in contemplation as she looked from it all and then back to him, but he watched her, trying to be patient even as he longed to return to his world and his time. This was all too much for one person to understand.

"You're never going to remember what all of this is for," she said finally, shaking her head. "I'll go back with you and help you recover. Then, if you can bring me back to the portal, I'll return home once again."

Dougal cleared his throat as he nodded his head. He hated having to ask for help, but he knew he needed her… and in more ways than she was referring to. Now that he knew she wasn't without her wits, he couldn't help himself from wanting to know more about her, and the thought of her leaving him now seemed unimaginable. When he looked at her, he saw a beautiful woman, yes, but he also saw... *his* woman. Whatever was supposed to happen between them, he was not ready to let her go, at least not yet.

Instead of saying anything however, he let her hold the bag while he wrapped his good arm around her waist, holding her close against him as they turned toward the shimmering light in the air.

She looked him in the eyes, nodding her head in an assent that all was right, and together they stepped into the portal, Dougal wrapping his arms around her once more as they spiralled through the darkness until they hit the ground once again.

## CHAPTER 13

Dougal opened his eyes much more tentatively this time, afraid of what he was going to find when he did. But there it all was – the battlegrounds as he had left them, the castle on the cliffs in good repair and bustling with people. Although nothing seemed more right than Emilia by his side. She helped him to the horses, seeming to understand that the portal had taken most of the strength he had left, although he tried to hide his weakness from her.

"I must change again," she said softly, and he nodded as he held onto his horse, watching her as she slipped behind the trees again, wishing, even as his strength ebbed, that he was in the copse with her.

Dougal couldn't have said exactly when or how, but everything between them had shifted. Perhaps it was that he now knew she spoke the truth. Or that they were the only two people who had experienced both the past and future and knew it was possible to move between them. Or maybe that he had trusted her as she had requested. Whatever it was, they couldn't seem to stop staring at one another, so much unspoken between them, neither of them willing to yet put it into words.

They mounted their horses and rode quickly back to his castle, nearly silent. Dougal let his horse make his own way on the familiar journey as he took strength from the woman by his side, much more grateful now and empathetic to what she was going through. She must be absolutely bewildered by the world she was now in. Yet she had stayed to see to his wounds and his health and now had returned to his world without even being asked – for him.

He didn't miss Emilia's worried looks, but he was grateful she didn't press him.

Once inside, they greeted the waiting Ivor before Dougal led Emilia to his bedchamber to tend to his wounds. Her hands were gentle, her cheeks pink as she touched him, and he couldn't help a bit of smugness knowing that he affected her in such a way.

Dougal didn't like the wince she tried to hide as she looked at the injury after removing the bandage. She cleaned it, then applied different creams and fresh bandages. The fabric was clean and the creams seemed to lessen the pain of the wounds.

"Here," she said, holding a strange pellet out toward him. "I have no idea what dosage to give you, but I can imagine that just a bit should do. These are small sample sizes so I'm hoping just a bit will make enough of a difference."

He nodded, trusting her as he swallowed them back.

Dougal couldn't stop staring at her as she worked on his arm, her touch both sure and hesitant at the same time. She seemed to know what she was doing, and yet was, apparently, as affected as he was as her fingers brushed against his skin. Yes, any man would want her for her beauty on first looking at her, but there was more there. She was brave, steady, sure, willing to give of herself to a man she hardly knew, who had been nothing but surly toward her. She cared about him, without knowing anything about him. She gave of herself for no reason at all.

Part of Dougal wanted to reach out and take her in his arms, offering her the comfort and kindness she deserved. The other part of him knew that to do so would be of detriment to them both. She was from another time and would be returning as soon as she deemed him healed. It almost made him want to keep the pain, if it meant she was would stay with him.

"Thank you," Dougal said in a soft tone, catching her hand. "I appreciate what ye've done for me."

She looked up, apparently startled at his sudden show of affection and gratitude. "You're welcome," she replied, softening her gaze, her eyes warm and steady.

For several moments they sat, staring at each other with hands clasped, content to simply be in this moment that fate or sorcery or God had given to them. Dougal longed for her in a way he never had for a woman before, and the vulnerability struck him as a weakness that would be of no use to a clan leader.

He needed a woman of this time and this place, someone to bear his children and take care of his family. This woman had another life waiting for her, and he couldn't bring himself to ask her to stay with him, knowing her answer would most likely be no.

Dougal had to stop this before anything began. He had no time for dreaming or wishing. He pulled his hand back and broke the eye contact, pushing himself to stand and walk to the window, crossing his arms over his chest. He didn't want her to leave but had no idea how else to keep himself from opening up to her more than he already had.

"You can leave now if you wish," he said gruffly. "Tell

A TIME TO LOVE

Arabel what she needs to do to look after the wound and I'll have my cousin take you back."

"So," she said, her voice smooth and soft. "The man of the last hour was too good to be true."

"You are from another world. You dinna belong here," he said, turning toward her with irritation, throwing his good arm out to the side. "What do you want of me?"

"I want nothing," she said, standing, finally showing some fire as her usually cool words were heated in answer to his anger. "I am only here, trying to save your life, and if I leave now surely you will die from an infection. Is that what you want?"

"Of course not, woman," he rebutted. "But I have many responsibilities here, and I canna have my mind on another mouth to feed."

"Fine then," she snapped. "Have it your way. Die if you want. Let it all be for naught. Your stubbornness is going to be the end of you."

She began cleaning up her supplies, her actions quick, heated, and Dougal found he couldn't watch her anymore, for all he wanted to do was rush toward her and apologize, asking her to stay. But it wasn't that easy. And so instead he turned to stare out the window, understanding that everything she was saying was the truth. Morag was fairly set in her ways and would never do as Emilia told her. She wouldn't take the consultation of another healer. Emilia could explain all to Arabel as he had suggested, but his sister would be so scared of failing him that she was more likely to do so in the process.

Like it or not, he needed Emilia, and he hated it. He wasn't a man who feared much, but his need for this woman, one he could never have, nearly terrified him. For years he had been pushed to marry, but never had he met a woman he could see as his wife. Until her.

He had so many responsibilities now that he was Laird, and having this on his mind could bring an end to it all. As much as he hated to admit it, he knew she was right. He had seen many men survive the battle only to die weeks later of a fever. Their limbs swelled up and festered. Some were lucky enough to just lose an arm, but most didn't make it even that far. She had knowledge from the future that could keep him from the same fate.

He had a family to think about. He had a clan to lead and to protect. Without him, it would be left to the elders until they either named an heir or let the clan fall to the dust. His family had worked too hard to keep the clan alive. His mother and father had lost their lives for it. He wasn't about to be the MacGavin that ended this legacy.

"Fine," he said gruffly in a low voice, not turning to look at her as he did. "Stay. You will need more clothing. Arabel will be in the kitchen. Ask her for it. Tell me when you need to see to my wounds, and I'll be there for you. Anything else you may need, ask my cousin."

With those words, Dougal turned and walked out of the room, avoiding looking at her. He pushed out the front door and made his way to the stables, where he stopped to catch his breath. He had agreed to keep her here with him, but he knew he needed to place as much distance between them as possible. There was something about Emilia that drew him in, made him want to be close to her. He couldn't allow himself to develop these feelings for her, not when he knew that she was going to leave.

Dougal looked up at the sky as the late afternoon sun beat down. This is what came of wandering after this strange woman. Half the day was gone and he needed to ensure the farming was done and food set out for supper.

Dougal stared back at the house, watching Arabel and his little cousins, sisters of Diarmid, take clothing off the lines and pile it into Emilia's arms. Her tousled, fiery red hair blew wildly in the wind as she laughed at something one of the children said.

Apparently sensing his stare, her head snapped up and found him across the field. He could just make out the troubled expression on her face before she turned her gaze away and forced the smile to return to her face at something his sister said. His heart stirred.

He didn't know what was going to come of this, except for one thing – it was going to spell trouble.

## CHAPTER 14

Emilia stood behind the tower house, staring out in the distance to where Dougal was helping to plow the fields. She leaned down and grabbed another tartan, hanging it from the line before wiping her hands on her apron. She had been in this time for a couple of weeks now and was beginning to become used to her daily routine. Without television, internet, or a library of books to occupy her time, she dove right into helping with the daily chores.

They washed and hung clothes, fed the horses, cooked the meals, and cleaned the house every day. The first couple of days were difficult, learning how to do everything without the help of machines or technological advances, but in the end, Emilia found the simplicity of it all very refreshing. She also enjoyed the time spent simply being with one another, conversing and enjoying each other's company, something they seemed to have lost in her own time.

The girls seemed very happy to have a woman in the household with them. Dougal's youngest cousin, Mattie, was six but laughed as she was the one teaching Emilia tasks that most here knew at such a young age. Six wasn't the same here as it was in the future. Emilia was saddened by the idea that these girls would never experience the carefree youth that she did at their age, although the stresses were so different. Arabel was already blossoming into a woman at the age of fifteen. She was strong and confident, and had obviously stepped into the role of woman of the house when her mother passed away.

When the chores were done and dinner was over, Emilia and Arabel would sit down in the chairs on the porch and talk about Arabel's future. She knew that she only had a couple of years at most before she was married off by her brother to another clansman, but she kept a high spirit about it, content in knowing her brother would do everything in his power to make sure she was well cared for.

As far as Dougal, Emilia only saw him for his treatment over the first couple of days, but as he grew more comfortable with her presence in the house, he began joining them for dinner and had even taken Emilia on a walk of the farm one late evening. She saw the gentle side of him again and realized that he could be charming and sweet when he wasn't trying to be the tough warrior and leader that everyone expected him to be. As much as she was pleased to see the improvement of his shoulder and the receding of the pain each day, Emilia's heart was torn in two at the thought of leaving him. He was as gruff and surly as ever, and wished she could see inside the man he was trying to hide from all.

It was late in the evening at the end of their second week together and Dougal had joined them at the kitchen table for supper. They sat together, listening to Dougal and Diarmid discuss how the farming was progressing, how one of the horses was expecting soon, and the changes that were taking place as Dougal assumed complete leadership. He was dedicated and honor bound to the role. Emilia could see that he took this responsibility to heart.

As the girls walked around the table after supper, cleaning up the dishes, Dougal leaned back and looked over at Emilia, catching her eye. She tried to smile at him, but his gaze was too intense, asked too much of her, and she couldn't find it within her to return, not here with the rest of his family sitting around them. Perhaps all that had been simmering between them would soon reach a head, but she didn't know how to face it, knowing that she would soon be leaving. Instead she pushed back her chair to rise and help clean, but Dougal reached up and gently tugged on her wrist, pulling her back down into the chair next to him.

"I have to go into Aberdeen tomorrow for provisions," he said quietly. "Would you join me?"

Arabel took Emilia's plate, looking down with a secret smile while Dougal's uncle and Diarmid looked up in surprise at his question. Why was it so important that she accompany him to town? He likely needed help with supplies. The thought of spending time alone with him, however, caused heat to spread from where he grasped her wrist.

Emilia had wanted to see Aberdeen in this time period before she returned, but her desire for Dougal was growing, as was the love for his family. She still didn't know quite how she felt about him besides her initial lust. There were moments when she saw beneath his bluster and cared deeply for him, but then he would do or say something to her that reminded her he was a hard man, not prone to show affection or vulnerability.

She took a deep breath, still unsure of how she was going to respond.

"I would love to," she said, surprised at her own words.

"Good. We will leave at sun's first light," he said with a terse smile toward her as he pushed back his chair and stood. "I'll have one of Mother's cloaks brought down so you can stay warm. Autumn is upon us, and the winds can get rough on the trip over."

"Thank you," Emilia responded, her eyes downcast.

After a near sleepless night that she spent tossing and turning, they left the next morning as the sun rose, riding next to each other along the muddy trail. Dougal was uncharacteristically chatty, asking Emilia all kinds of questions about her world and even laughed when she told him a bit about the history of America, a land he knew nothing about. He was fascinated about all that was to be discovered.

The technological advances were more than he could grasp, the idea of an electric toothbrush more exciting to him than the telephone, a concept he could not quite understand — not that Emilia expected him to.

Upon her arrival, she had kept her knowledge of the future to herself, unsure of how sharing it would change anything. When they had returned to her time, however, she had been astonished to find everything was unchanged, that her return to the past had caused no ripple to the recorded history of this time period or anything beyond it. She had even picked up the one book from the library that she knew contained mention of the MacGavins, and found nothing out of the ordinary. It was as if her return had been pre-destined and already written into history.

They conversed the entire distance to Aberdeen and when they arrived there was a warmth about her heart, and she smiled at him and their newfound knowledge of one another.

Once they dismounted in town, Emilia walked quietly beside him, nodding to the people walking in the street. She waited patiently as he went into the stores he needed, traded for the goods required, and loaded them onto their horses. As they approached the edge of town, he stopped, looking up at a small building.

"Wait here for me." He seemed to be anticipating something, but Emilia didn't ask questions as he left her and ran inside.

Emilia stood in the street watching as the people milled through the town, talking to each other, shopping, and going to their respective jobs. In reality, things weren't that much different in her own time, except that perhaps in the future there was less camaraderie, more people in a hurry as they rushed from one event to the next. She supposed that equipment and technology had changed, but the general human nature of people stayed the same. She smiled as she took in the people in the small town, enjoying each moment for what it was.

"You look like you belong here," a voice said from behind her. Emilia whirled around and blinked, shocked at the sight of the woman from her own time, Fiona, standing behind her with a smile on her face.

"Fiona!" Emilia said with excitement and awe. "What are you doing here? Did you come through the portal as well?"

"You're an interesting girl," Fiona said, looking Emilia up and down as if she hadn't heard her question. "You know, the portal, it is a natural thing. It's nature's way of working out the kinks in history. Every person given passage through that portal is written in the cosmic pages of time."

"I'm not sure I understand," Emilia replied, slowly realizing that perhaps Fiona had more to do with this than she had originally assumed. "How does it work? What do you know of it? Do you control it?"

"In a way," she smiled, in a singsong voice. "Just remember that your decisions here will affect only *your* future. Follow your heart. It will never lead you astray."

Emilia looked over as Dougal walked out of the shop carrying a small box that he placed in the satchel on the side of the horse. She turned back toward Fiona but she was gone, no trace of her anywhere. Emilia let out a groan and kicked at a rock beneath her feet, frustrated with the mysterious woman who she now realized was part of it all, if not the orchestrator. It seemed, however, that the woman came and went as she pleased, so Emilia had no way of reaching her again, even if she wanted to. Instead, she turned back to Dougal, who actually smiled at her as he helped her up onto the horse.

Their return ride was a quieter one and Emilia contemplated her next course of action. Had she been sent here to ensure Dougal's survival, and therefore that of the MacGavin clan? Was that why the history books were murky — because her existence was one that couldn't be explained through history as she knew it? As a historian, she knew better than anyone that one action led to another, and yet when she had seen Dougal lying in that field she couldn't help but do all she could to save him.

And despite what she had done, nothing had changed in the future and, in fact, Dougal likely would have died had she not been there. How strange.

When they returned home and unpacked their supplies, the castle was quiet, the children and Arabel already in bed.

Emilia began to walk to her own chamber, when Dougal reached out a hand, placing it on her arm to stop her.

"Sit with me for a moment?"

She hesitated. She had come to a decision, and it was one she could no longer avoid. She should be putting as much space between them as possible and yet… she couldn't help but nod and follow him to the fire in the great hearth, taking a seat on the deerskin rug, welcoming the warmth as they watched the flickering light in silence. The flames were bright and vibrant, casting shadows across the room. Emilia knew her time here was over. They both knew it — she could feel the unspoken words between them. Actually saying them to him out loud was the hard part.

"Dougal," she finally said, looking over at him. "I am planning to leave tomorrow. You are well now and have no need of my knowledge any longer."

"I figured that was coming," he said with a remorseful smile, moving over next to her on the deerskin rug. "I have something for you. Something for you to take with you on your return, to remember us by."

Dougal handed her the small box she had seen him purchase from the store in Aberdeen. She carefully opened the hinged golden box. Inside was a silver locket, etched with the date. She gasped and pulled it from the box, opening it to find rose petals clasped inside. Dougal took it from her hands and instead of turning her around, he wrapped his arms around her neck, fastening it under her hair.

"I hope this brings you luck. Roses will always remind me of you," he whispered, his face now very close to hers. "They're your scent."

Emilia didn't think, but just acted. She leaned forward and pressed her lips against his, her resolve burned down like the heat of the fire.

Dougal instantly responded, his arms wrapping around her and pulling her in close against his chest. The heat from his skin radiated onto her and she could feel her breasts heave overtop her racing heart. Kissing him set off an explosion in her chest, and as his hands ran down the back of her dress, the space between her legs ached fiercely for him. Without a word, Dougal tugged at the ribbons on the back of her gown, pulling the shoulders down and kissing her neck. Passion erupted as he pushed her back, pulling the dress down her body and tossing it to the side, exposing her body to him. She hadn't gotten the hang of her undergarments yet so she lay on the soft rug, waiting,

# A TIME TO LOVE

as his eyes hungrily, greedily roved up and down over top of her.

He stood up, leaned down, and picked her up, cradling her in his arms as he walked her back out of the great hall and up the stairs to his chamber. The blaze of the fireplace was just as romantic, and Emilia groaned as he laid her gently down on his bed. She watched as he unbuckled his belt and yanked his boots off before dropping his kilt to the floor. Her eyes widened as it revealed the length of him, standing at attention for her beneath the fabric. He looked down at her with darkened eyes, passion flowing from every pore as he climbed across the bed and sank down on top of her. This was a man who did nothing without purpose.

Their lips met again, but this time with an indescribable need, and Emilia ran her hands over his chest and down to his manhood. He groaned into her mouth as she clasped her hand around his shaft and slowly began to move it up and down, already desperate for him to be inside of her.

They kissed passionately as his hands slipped down Emilia's body to where she was aching for him. Two fingers slipped through her folds and caressed her first gently and then with greater urgency as she moaned with need of him. His thumb moved over her center, circling around it with heated aggression and she could feel an orgasm already simmering in her belly. She arched her back and spread her legs wider as he began to breathe heavily, circling his thumb around and pushing his fingers even deeper inside of her. She gripped on tightly to him and stared into his wanting eyes.

"I need you inside of me," she whispered.

"Are you certain?" he whispered huskily, and she nodded.

"I've never been surer of anything."

He pulled his fingers out and moved over top of her, allowing her to guide him toward her, and then pushed softly into her. She gasped as he filled her up, feeling every inch of him seeming to expand within her and pulsate inside. He groaned, grasping the sheets as he moved his hips slowly back and forth, sliding in and out as the waves of pleasure within Emilia began to rise even higher.

He pulled her hips up to take him deeper, and she wrapped her legs around his waist. He reached down and grabbed her thigh, pulling her body upwards as he thrust. Shadows of their intertwined bodies moved across the ceiling in the light of the fire, and Emilia stifled a deep groan as he pulled her closer and closer.

She began to move her hips against him, pushing forward as he thrust deep. Her lust turned to pure need and they both picked up the pace, feeling themselves lost in each other's touch. The sounds of their skin colliding echoed through the room, and Emilia grabbed onto his shoulders as his body moved over her like waves.

Emilia could hear the need in his breath as she began to writhe underneath him, trying to hold back just a bit longer, to enjoy this even more. As he reached down and held her hips, however, slapping his body hard against hers, she released her control and erupted, pressing her mouth against his and moaning into it.

Her explosion seemed to drive him over the edge, and Emilia could feel Dougal's shoulders tense as he thrust one more time, pushing in deep and groaning loudly as he released his seed. His cock pulsated over and over again inside of Emilia as her own orgasm was heightened by his. Their bodies stilled, arched together as they allowed the waves to wash over them.

Slowly she became aware of his body releasing as he continued to move his hips in short, steady bursts. She collapsed down on the bed, sweating from the encounter, breathing heavy with emotion. Dougal leaned down and kissed her lips softly before moving to the side and laying his body next to hers. Her lips curled in satisfaction as he turned her onto her side and wrapped his large arms around her, pulling her in close. He lifted the soft fur covers over them and they laid there silently, reveling in their bond, one of his arms underneath her head and the other stroking her hair back, away from her face.

It was too much. Emilia closed her eyes, the emotions of the evening overwhelming her, and she listened as his breath slowed until his hand stilled as he fell into a deep sleep.

Emilia grasped onto his hands, letting the tears start to fall. How could she leave this man tomorrow, after all that had happened to them, of the joining they had just had, more intimate than any she had ever known before?

She could never stay — could she? Was she even supposed to have come? She wished she could have had more time with Fiona so that she could try to understand what was happening to her. Emilia opened her eyes and stared out the window at the twinkling night sky. Taking in a deep breath, she resolved to enjoy this moment, as they would be a few of her last with Dougal. Her fingertips moved over the locket still around her neck and she squeezed it, knowing that she would at least be able to take a piece of him with her when she left. Perhaps he would give her a lock of hair to lay beside the rose petals.

Holding onto him with a desperation she didn't know she possessed, Emilia slowly drifted into a deep sleep, hoping and praying the daylight would bring her some sort of reprieve from this breaking of her heart.

## CHAPTER 15

The sun peeking over the horizon and through the windows woke Dougal from his deep sleep. He kept his eyes firmly shut, however, not quite ready to face this new day – not when it was the day that would take Emilia away from him.

He turned over in the bed and reached for her, anticipating her soft warm skin against his fingertips, her taste still on his lips. His eyes sprung open when he felt nothing but blankets, dismayed to find her gone, the room empty and quiet. Dougal rolled onto his back, his arm coming to rest on his forehead as he prayed she had just risen early to help the girls and had not taken on some self-sacrificial mission and returned to the portal without a word of goodbye to him.

He forced himself out of bed and dressed, the sweet scent of rose still filling the air as he tried to ignore the growing knot in the pit of his stomach. He opened the door to nothing but silence in the hall and continued his search in the kitchen. The room was empty of both people and any breakfast preparations, so he turned and made his way to the great hall. The dress he had stripped from her body last night was no longer on the floor, telling him that she had, at least, been here since last night.

Frustration building inside of him at her complete disappearance, he walked to her bedroom and knocked before he opened the door. The room was empty and the bed was still made from the day before – so she hadn't snuck back here during the night.

The panicky knot grew to fear surging through his chest, and his feet quickened into a run as he checked every room without luck. How could she leave him, just like that, after such a night together? She was scared, he knew that, but to disappear without a word was incomprehensible.

Dougal was determined now that there was no way he would allow her to simply walk out of his life like that, without a word to him. He ran back to his room and threw on his belt and sashes. He pulled his hair back from his face and lifted his cloak from the chair. If her intention was to return to the portal, he should be able to ride hard enough to head her off before she reached it.

The realization hit him with as much shock as the portal itself had. He had no intention of letting her leave. He could no longer imagine life without her by his side, and there was certainly no other woman who could ever take her place.

Even if he had to return to her world to look for her, he would do it. He would face the monstrous beasts, the towering structures, the painted world, in order to find her and convince her to return with him. And if she wouldn't… well, he would have a choice to make.

Dougal sheathed his sword and turned to the door, walking straight past his cousin who was standing in the hall, having appeared at some point while Dougal was concocting his plans. Dougal had no time to speak to Diarmid – there would be time for that later. At the moment, he had to get to that shimmering light, no matter what it took.

If it disappeared and he never saw Emilia again? No, he couldn't allow the thought. Dougal brushed past his cousin, who was calling out his name, trying to capture his attention. He waved him off, not having the time to answer any questions. Dougal reached for the doorlatch, but before he could leave, his cousin's hand clasped his shoulder. Diarmid should know well enough to leave off when Dougal was in an angry spell, and he spun around to face him, wondering what could be so important.

"Diarmid, I dinna have time for this," he said abruptly, trying to turn toward the door. "I must find Emilia. She has left for her home, and I must stop her before I am never able to find her again."

"Dougal," Diarmid said desperately. "That's just it. Emilia hasna left for home. She has been taken."

That stopped Dougal, and he turned back around. "What? Why would you say such a thing?"

"This was pinned to the door with a Buchanan tartan," he said, holding up the necklace Dougal had given her just last night. "I can only assume it to be Emilia's as I've never seen one of the other girls wearing it. She had gone out to the berry patch for breakfast but never returned. When I came back from the stables, this was on the door."

Dougal reached over and carefully took the locket, squeezing it in his fist, the point of the heart digging into his palm, but he welcomed the pain. He closed his eyes and tried to center his anger, knowing that exploding at that moment wasn't going to get Emilia back.

Alastair had gone too far this time, and he had aggrieved the wrong laird. Dougal had known retribution was coming, but to take Emilia from him… Dougal fought the instinct to run to the stables, mount his horse, and go after the Buchanans himself. That would only result in the deaths of both him and Emilia. He needed the help of his clan.

Instead, he slammed the front door shut and slowly walked into the living area, staring into the fire as the old flame of revenge burnt bright within him. He had to make a plan and get her back before the Buchanans did so much damage that Emilia would never be the same, or worse, before Alastair slit her throat and left her for dead.

"Gather the elders and the soldiers," he commanded to his cousin. "We need a plan and we need one quickly."

"Aye, Dougal," Diarmid said, bowing and running from the room.

Dougal turned and walked toward the window, staring out as Diarmid raced for the stables, jumped on a horse, and sped down the road. The sky was dark and gray and Dougal could feel a storm brewing overhead, echoing that which filled him as the desperation grew. From behind him, he could hear the whines and sniffles of his sister and cousins, who had entered the castle from wherever they had apparently been searching for Emilia. He regretted they had heard the trouble and felt a bit guilty that they had heard his own rage, but so be it – they would have to come to terms with what was about to happen.

He took a breath, remembering all he had a responsibility to and thinking of what Emilia herself would do in such a situation, before he turned and knelt down, allowing them at least the comfort of his arms. They had fallen in love with Emilia, and this was too much of a resemblance to their own mothers' deaths. Arabel sniffed back her tears, asking what she could do to stay busy, and Dougal suggested they prepare food for the coming elders and clansmen. After a long, agonizing hour, Diarmid rounded the corner and trooped up the walk from the stables, Ivor and the elders following soon behind. Dougal quickly walked to the door and welcomed them inside before seating them at the hall's long, narrow table.

Once they were assembled, however Dougal found he couldn't sit still and instead began pacing the room. He couldn't let anything happen to Emilia, regardless of whether she went back to her time or not. Even if she left him, at least he would know that she was out there, free to live the life she chose.

Dougal had never loved a woman before… had never let anyone into his heart. He hadn't exactly welcomed Emilia either, but somehow, she had made her way in despite him. The others talked amongst themselves as Dougal imagined Alastair bleeding from the throat after he sliced his knife across his skin. This had gone on long enough.

"We need to go after her, and soon," Ivor said. "She saved Dougal's life, and now we repay that."

"But she is not family," one of the elders said, speaking up. "Do we risk the safety of our clan for an outsider?"

"This is not up for debate." Dougal finally lost his temper, storming over to the table and slamming one fist down upon it. "You are no longer in charge of this clan. I am. The woman is in danger and she was taken from our home in retribution for our clan's actions against them, not because of anything she did. It is our responsibility to do all we can to keep her safe and alive. Consider the dishonor the Buchanan has shown us yet again. Alastair has played around the rules for far too long as we sat back and took our time. Now he has come into my home and taken what is mine. For that, he will pay."

"Wait a moment, son," an elder protested. "Starting a clan war is serious and must be determined by all members."

"I can speak for the entirety of my family," Ivor said, standing up. "We stand behind the Laird's decision. And if ye think the rest would back down, you have severely underestimated the loyalty we have to Dougal MacGavin. I willna allow that girl's blood to be on our hands."

A TIME TO LOVE

Dougal nodded at Ivor, who returned the gesture with the slightest tilt of his head. The elders looked at one another and then back at Dougal.

"Tell me Dougal," said Leonis, leaning back in his chair, eyeing Dougal shrewdly. "You call this woman 'yours.' Have you made your choice then? Is she to be your wife?"

Ivor's head swiveled around to look at his friend, and Dougal took a breath as all eyes were on him once more.

"I... I suppose she will," said Dougal, nodding, swallowing the doubt that filled him at what she might have to say about it. "If she'll have me."

The elders looked at him incredulously. What girl would *not* marry the laird of a powerful Highland clan? That Dougal should leave the choice to the woman was beyond them, which Dougal understood. But they didn't know Emilia like he did. She was independent and sure of herself and nearly as stubborn as he was when she thought she was right. And he wouldn't have it – or her – any other way.

Dougal clapped his hands and sat down at the table, ready to make plans with Ivor. As they sat there preparing their attack, the others trickled in to be apprised of the situation and learn the strategy of the rescue attempt.

It was at that moment that Dougal realized he had finally come into his own as a leader and his clan was committed to supporting him, regardless of what the elders said. Even his uncle, who hadn't exactly been pleased with being relieved of his Master of the House duties, came strolling through the door, ready to offer his advice. He hated Alastair as much as, if not more so, than Dougal did and would like nothing more than to see him dead.

After they determined logistics, the men stood and went their separate ways to gather supplies, ready their horses, and prepare for battle. As Dougal stood at his window staring out at the clan working together for this cause, pride in his people and worry for Emilia warred with one another for his attention.

His clansmen were thinking beyond their own bloodline. Too many times people's lives were wasted because clans were so simple minded that they refused to see beyond their own surname. As Dougal stepped into his new role, he was making damn sure that the MacGavins would not go down in history as a clan only worried of self-preservation.

But perhaps Emilia was the one who would make all of the difference for their future.

As he allowed his thoughts to refocus on Emilia, he took a deep breath, filling his lungs before letting it out slowly. He had to believe that they were not too late, that she would be there waiting for them – and willing to become his.

## CHAPTER 16

Her arms were tied behind her back and her mouth was gagged as she sat on display in a wooden chair in the great room of a castle similar to that of the MacGavins. This, however, was far more elaborate, built to impress more than protect.

Emilia's eyes darted nervously back and forth across the room, landing on Alastair Buchanan laughing maniacally where he was surrounded by his fellow clansmen. Emilia didn't know what he wanted or why he had taken her, but she was terrified beyond any fear she had ever known before. She knew as well as anyone that this man had no qualms about killing a prisoner who was no longer of any use to him. She would be no different. She had to determine his purpose for her, as the only way she could see out of this was to somehow convince him to let her go.

When Emilia had woken that morning, she had turned over in bed and ran her hands across Dougal's chest, stopping them over his heart, beating under the warmth of his skin. She had leaned forward, placing her chin on her hands as she stared up at him, his face still hard even in repose, as though the weight of his responsibilities stayed on his mind even as he slept.

She sighed as she realized that she was completely smitten, wanting to be nowhere else than where she had spent the night, wrapped in his arms, with his hard body pressed against her as his arms held her close.

She had tried so hard to avoid feeling anything for him, and yet here she was, falling for a sixteenth century Highlander warrior. What she was supposed to do about that, she had no idea.

Her future – or past? – could look so incredibly different. She had thought today would be the day she would return home, back to the 21$^{st}$ century. And yet… her heart twisted and she realized just how desperately she wanted to stay.

She had spent so many years studying this land and this time that it almost seemed familiar to her. She had always been so lost in the past that now that it was her reality it didn't seem that strange at all. How was she supposed to return, only to spend her life studying this time that she had come to know so intimately, with all of the people she had come to consider as family lost to her in the history of this time? For when she thought about what mattered, it was the man lying next to her.

When she had first met him, he had been so angry and so rude. While she understood that his anger and stoicism would always be a part of him, she saw so much more than that. She saw a man who loved his family, a man who would do anything to protect his clan. He was a fierce warrior, a brave leader, and yet had also shown her vulnerability and kindness.

She had snuck out of the bed as her musings had kept her from sleep and she wanted to let Dougal sleep. She decided she would cook him breakfast and bring it back to bed, where she could take her time feeding it to him. Perhaps

A TIME TO LOVE

pancakes were in order. Hopefully they would have enough in the kitchens she could make them out of something other than barley flour. After checking the stores, she decided to pick berries from the bushes in back of the castle.

Emilia was so used to people coming and going from the farm that she paid no attention to the two men arriving on foot from the back road. She hummed to herself as she picked the berries and piled them into her apron, her mind returning to the night before and the love she and Dougal had made in the light of the fire.

She thought about what Fiona had said about following her heart and that if she truly did so, she would end up exactly where she was supposed to be. Today, her heart was leading her right back into Dougal's arms. What harm could there be in staying at least another day until she could figure out whether she truly wanted to remain in this century, or if it was the residual pleasure from the lovemaking that was leading her decision?

She reached for another berry and paused, feeling a presence behind her. Before she could turn, an arm snaked around her waist and a hand pressed against her mouth, silencing her. Emilia dropped the berries on the ground and flailed wildly, trying to escape from whoever was holding onto her, but the strength in the arms that gripped her was too great to fight.

Emilia was carried down to the edge of the tree line and out to the road, where her hands were tied behind her back and she was dropped in the back of a wagon. She looked around, desperately trying to see the culprits, but the world went dark when they threw a blanket over her head before she could get a good look. She managed to work it off by the time they walked her into the Buchanan estate, as she immediately recognized the flags.

Visions of their soldiers lying dead in the fields surged

through her brain. Were they going to kill her in revenge? Was she just a pawn in their attempt to get back at the MacGavin Clan? Would Dougal even know she was gone? She tried to focus on the cool metal of the chain locket against the back of her neck but, felling nothing, she looked down, seeing that it had been taken. She began to panic as the clansman laughed, speaking in Gaelic about how satisfied their laird would be with their prize.

Alastair now slowly approached her, rubbing his hands together. He leaned down close to her face, his foul breath stinging her nostrils. She turned her head away from his but he grabbed her face with his hands and turned it toward him. He stared at her with his beady dark eyes and scruffy red beard, smiling as he obviously sensed her fear.

"Do you think your precious Dougal will come to rescue you?"

She refused to answer his question, but met his eyes, narrowing them angrily at him.

"That means he will. Good," he said, smiling a wicked grin. "It will make things so much easier when he comes to me. But don't worry my dear, when I kill him, I'll make sure to throw yer body in the pit next to his."

Thankfully, it seemed that the Buchanan men had misjudged her and not tied her hands tightly enough, and Emilia had been able to work at the rope around her hands on the wagon ride over. She lifted one of her freed hands, slapping Alastair as hard as she could across the face. She tried to stand but before she could, three men grabbed her and held her forcibly down in the chair.

Alastair pulled a white handkerchief from his belt and wiped his bloody lip, an evil smirk pulling at his lips. He took slow steps toward her, his smile fading, only to be replaced by a sinister look that caused the panic within Emilia to grow. He reached out suddenly, grabbing Emilia by the throat and squeezing. She scrambled, trying to break free by scratching at his hands around her neck, but she began to weaken as she struggled for breath.

"Perhaps I willna kill you right away," he said through gritted teeth. "Maybe we'll have some fun with you first. And if that don' kill you then I'll make sure to finish ye off myself."

He let go of her throat and she wheezed and hissed through the cloth that had been stretched over her mouth. Everything in her urged her to fight harder against him, but she knew it would only cause her more pain for little use. Emilia took a long, shuddering breath, as she tried to prevent the fear that was choking her from showing on her face. She didn't want to give Alastair the satisfaction. He laughed as he caught her glare.

"Throw her in the storeroom," he said, waving his bloody handkerchief. "Leave her as bait for the MacGavin. Then we will circle him from behind."

The men picked her up out of the chair and carried her by the arms down the hall and to a small room at the end. Emilia protested through the gag as they tossed her onto the cold hard floor and slammed the door shut. She jumped up, grabbing the doorlatch but the door wouldn't budge. As she cried out, banging on the door, men laughed on the other side, the sound slowly receding as they apparently returned to their clan.

Emilia yanked the gag from her mouth and turned in slow circles, searching out anything that might help her, but the room was so dark she could barely see her hand in front of her face.

She wrapped her arms around herself, her chest flooded with fear. There didn't seem to be an ounce of humanity left in these men and she knew if things went bad for Dougal, she would never make it out of here alive. No one would ever know what happened to her. She would have simply disappeared, lost in another time, a time where she didn't exist. Her greatest fear now was that Dougal might sacrifice himself trying to save her. Even if he didn't care for her as she did for him, she knew that his sense of honor would never allow him to leave her to face the Buchanans alone.

And if the Buchanans caught him in their trap... Arabel would be left to fend for herself, the MacGavins would not only lose their best men but also their leader, and the clan would be left in disarray. Everything in their future hinged on Dougal's survival.

She should have walked away when she had the chance. What if her presence here changed everything for the Buchanans? The historian in her had told her to leave, but the woman she was had convinced her to stay.

Tears welled up in her eyes as she pounded on the wall in frustration as Dougal filled her mind. He was so strong, so obstinate, and yet so loyal and loving beneath all of the bluster. He was everything she had ever wanted but hadn't known she needed. Little did she know that all of the research, all of the studying that had filled her life in the future had been preparing her to meet him. Now, however, she didn't even know if she would make it out of this house alive, much less ever know the comforting warmth of his embrace again. Was she to come all this way only to have felt his love the one time?

She shook her head, wondering how she had gone from the young new history professor at NYU to a lost girl in the very time period she specialized in. How anticlimactic could one life be? For several minutes, she let the emotions flood her system and spill out of her eyes.

She sobbed in fear of dying, in fear that Dougal would be killed, for lost love, and for the utter helplessness that washed over her. Why had she been shown a portal if it was going to end like this? How had she changed history at all? Emilia thought of Fiona sitting next to her on the plane, then in the café, and finally in the town itself here in this century, orchestrating all of this like a twisted fairy godmother. Emilia looked up into the darkness, wiping the tears from eyes and wondering if Fiona could hear her.

"Fiona," she said, softly at first, then waited a moment and repeated her name, more loudly this time. "Fiona. I need you. Now more than ever. Please!"

She sat still, waiting for a response but still there was nothing. She felt stupid, realizing this was ludicrous and she was really just sitting here talking to herself. Either way, she had nothing to lose, so she took a deep breath and pulled herself to her feet.

"Fiona!" she yelled out. "Tell me what to do. I followed my heart just like you told me, and it has led me here."

Still, she heard and saw nothing but silence. Emilia slunk back against the wall, sliding down and pulling her knees to her chest. She wasn't sure what else to do. She did not want to die alone in this dank storeroom, or even worse at the hands of the Buchanan men. Emilia was not naive and she had far too much knowledge of the history of this clan and their brutality.

She lay her head on her knees in defeat, but then felt a strange energy moving through her chest. She picked up her head and sniffed, looking around for any sign that her desperate attempt to contact a fairy godmother actually worked. It sounded preposterous, and yet, here she was, in 1545.

She must have been making up the feeling, Emilia thought when the only thing surrounding her was silence.

"He's coming," a voice whispered suddenly through the air. Emilia swiveled her head around, searching for its source.

"What?"

"He's coming," Fiona said in her head, her voice firm this time. Emilia saw nothing change in the room, but she knew for a fact the voice had come clearly through her consciousness. The whisper repeated. Emilia's pulse raced as she impatiently waited for something, anything, to happen.

She jumped when she did hear the sound of crashing and yelling. She threw herself back against the wall, listening to men screaming their war cry, followed by the clashing of swords. It sounded like there was a fight ensuing on the other side. Dougal coming for her was both an answer to her prayers and her worst nightmare.

Emilia stood at the back of the room and stared at the door, wishing she could see what was going on behind it. She didn't know whose screams were whose and the sound of the sword fight sent shivers down her spine. It was one thing to study such battles and another thing to live them.

The MacGavins deserved great honor and a strong and robust future. Should she live through this, she vowed to ensure they would receive their rightful place in history. She would note it all in detail, through the eyes of a historian, to ensure their legacy lived forever.

The true question was – was she here to save or ruin the MacGavin legacy?

## CHAPTER 17

As Dougal raced his horse to the home of the Buchanan laird, the only thought running through his mind was that Emilia better be alive when he arrived or he would destroy the Buchanan's entire castle with Alastair and all his men inside of it.

The thought of losing Emilia sent a chill through him, an ache through his chest that he tried to ignore as he continued to push his horse as fast as he could run. Dougal knew the Buchanans wanted him, and their spy had likely determined that Emilia was one of his weaknesses. He had been too soft – he should have killed the man.

This is why the Buchanans had been quiet. They had been watching, waiting, finding the perfect moment to exact revenge. Dougal had ensured his own lands were so well protected, they had chosen to draw him out instead. He should have been ready, watching. But between his days of recovery from his wound and his focus on Emilia, he had missed the signs.

He had been right to try to push Emilia away – she had made him vulnerable, as he had feared. They had used her against him, and now he had to face the idea of losing her, as he risked his own men.

The MacGavins rode through the keep to the base of the steps of the castle leading to the massive front doors. The castle wasn't as well protected as Dougal's own, and the MacGavins easily – perhaps too easily – overtook the small number of men who were keeping watch.

When they reached the front doors, Dougal looked at his men and nodded in confidence. Ivor came forward and with one great bellow and straining biceps, tore the doors right off their hinges. Dougal had seen Ivor accomplish some impressive feats before, but this was nearly beyond human. The Buchanans were ready for a fight, and the MacGavins had brought it right to Alastair's front door. As soon as the doors went crashing to the ground, the clansmen inside dispersed in panic.

Dougal watched in disgust as Alastair slunk behind his men, a few of them surrounding him to protect him. The MacGavins pulled out their swords and began the attack, clashing against the unsuspecting men. They had known Dougal would come, but likely hadn't realized he would come so quickly or with such a backing from his men. As Dougal moved through the crowd, wrestling men to the ground, using his sword without mercy, he looked down the hall at the closed door at the end, which was protected by a small amount of Buchanans. That must be where they were keeping Emilia, but he wouldn't go after her until it was safe.

Dougal looked over at Ivor as he thrust a man against the wall, shoving his dagger into his stomach and then retracting, letting him fall into a pile on the floor. Ivor smiled at Dougal as he grabbed another clansman by the hair, pulling his head back and slitting his throat. Dougal shook his head in admiration as he blocked a blow from the man standing to his left, turning and kicking him hard in the stomach.

The man fell back against the others, toppling them over into a pile. Dougal took that moment to push forward, seeking out Alistair. One by one, he sent his men charging at Dougal, fear flashing in his eyes as Dougal made quick work of them. Blood seeped through the cracks in the wood floors, trickling up to the edge of Alastair's boots. He growled loudly as he pushed his last two men toward Dougal, their hands shaking as they approached. They circled around him slowly, but Dougal had no time to draw this out. As one attacked, Dougal sliced his sword across the man's hand and took both of them out at once, leaving Alistair finally unprotected when they fell to the floor.

"Ahhh," Alastair bellowed, pulling his sword from his side. "You fool. I will have your head for this and the head of your dear little sister. After that I will keep your whore and use her myself."

Alastair lunged forward with his sword, but missed as Dougal dodged to the left. Alastair flew forward into the table, knocking his vases full of whiskey to the ground. He smiled coyly as he tossed his graying red hair behind him and straightened his kilt. He crouched, deciding to take a different approach, which was ridiculous as Dougal could see every move before he made it. Alastair had been able to pay for the largest and best-trained army, but had never been much of a warrior himself. When Alastair missed him once again, Dougal pulled out his dagger and sliced him across the face. Alastair grabbed his cheek and looked up at Dougal, a manic look in his eyes as he laughed.

"When yer father died," he said breathlessly. "He begged for mercy. He cried out in shame."

Anger simmered deep in Dougal's chest at the mention of his father. He had been a proud man and a strong warrior, and Dougal knew Alastair's words were lies. Nonetheless, it angered him worse than anything Alastair could have spoken. Dougal walked forward, raising his sword and lunging, stopping inches from Alastair's face. Alastair winced, slowly opening his eyes as Dougal began to smile.

"Ye'er not worth my time," Dougal said, lowering his sword. "You deserve death, but even more so, you deserve for yer name and yer clan's to lose any respect you might have had. You will leave this land and never return, do you understand me? You will take all of the Buchanans. You may still lead them Alastair, but lead them away from here. If I ever see any of you here again, I will take your head clear off yer shoulders."

Alastair nodded, dropping his dagger to his belt. The fear in his eyes told Dougal everything he needed to know. Ridding the Highlands of the Buchanans was worth the sacrifice of not being the one to end Alistair's life.

Dougal turned, more ready than ever to find Emilia and tell her exactly what he felt for her, but Ivor's cry of warning had him turning, his body already prepared for the attack to come.

Dougal turned just in time to catch Alastair's maniacal grin as he ran toward Dougal, his sword held high. Dougal swiftly pulled his dagger from his belt and stepped to the side in the same motion as he lifted the weapon and plunged it deep into Alastair's heart. Alistair's sword clattered to the ground as he fell into Dougal, gasping for breath. Dougal dropped him on the floor and wiped his dagger on his shirt. He pulled his sword from its sheath and held it high over his head.

"You will never learn," he said, shaking his head and bringing his sword down hard and swift, ending Alastair Buchanan's life.

Silence filled the room as his head rolled across the floor. Dougal turned to find the Buchanan clan staring at them, eyes wide. One by one, they dropped their weapons and ran from the house, their pay and motivations disappeared with their leader. Despite his best attempts, Alastair Buchanan had no heirs to his clan, which could only mean one thing – the long-standing feud between the Buchanans and the MacGavins was finally over.

Dougal breathed heavily, stunned into silence, until Ivor's roar of victory rung out and the rest of the MacGavins let out a cheer as they slapped one another on the backs in congratulations. They tried to lift Dougal into the air, but he shook his head as he pushed past them. Time for celebration would come later. He had something else to see to first. He tossed his sword to Ivor and pushed past the others, his feet quickening into a run as he approached the end of the hallway and flung the storeroom door open, searching through the darkness.

Please let her be here. Please let her be untouched, unharmed. Please—

And there she was. Emilia stood across from him in the corner of the closet, her hands plastered on the wall behind her, her face tight in fear. When she saw Dougal, she pushed away from the wall and they met in the middle of the room as he had moved toward her without thought, and she threw her body against his.

He wrapped his arms around her tightly, lifting her in the air as he vowed to never let any danger befall her again. She was his weakness, yes. But, he realized, she was also his strength. They had defeated the Buchanans with such ferocity only because of how intent he had been to find her. His mouth fused against hers as they kissed with the desperation that they had felt at the possibility of never seeing one another again. Dougal had pushed aside the fear that had filled him, but now that she was here in his arms, he finally allowed himself to realize just how terrified he had been that she might not be here, waiting for him, as eager to see him again as he was her.

He finally pulled back and looked into her face, at the tears running down her cheeks, her hair a mess around her head. The skin about her wrists was chafed and bleeding from rope burns, while her neck was covered in bruises. He wished now that Alastair was still alive so that he could kill him all over again for putting his hands on his woman.

Dougal took Emilia by the shoulders, staring at her in wonder. She wiped the tears from her face and sniffed as she peered up at him, biting her lip with some hesitancy. Dougal couldn't even begin to think of a world without her. She had become everything to him, and there was no other woman he would share his life with. If she didn't want him, then so be it. He would spend the rest of his life alone.

"Emilia, I'm so sorry," he said, lifting his hand and wiping the one remaining tear. "This was all my fault. Did he hurt you? Did he—"

"No," she said, cutting him off as she shook his head. "I'm fine. It was my fault, Dougal. If it wasn't for me, if I wasn't here, you never would have—"

"Dinna say that," he said forcefully. "Never say that you shouldna be here, that you dinna belong here. You belong with me, Emilia. It doesna matter what your history or your books tell you. You are mine, and you always will be, do you hear me?"

"Dougal—"

She couldn't say she was going to leave him. He wouldn't let her.

"If you choose to go back, then go back," he said, staring deeply into her eyes so that she would understand his intention. "But then I am going with you."

"You hated my time!" she protested, even as her eyes lit up. "And your clan, your leadership, your responsibility—"

"It doesna matter. For I would have you. I love you, Emilia," he confessed, the words coming from deep inside of him. "More than anything in my life. I will do anything to be with you."

"I love you, too, Dougal," she cried, another tear forming in her eye. "With all of my being."

"I know you are from another time, another place," he said as he gently brushed away her tears. "Yet I feel that we've been pulled together from ages apart to find one another. For so long something has been missing in my life, and I thought it was becoming the true laird of the MacGavins. But it was you I was waiting for. Should ye wish to return to the land ye call home, we will make it so. I will fight the metal beasts that carry people, and I will gather my food from the supply store rather than the fields and the forests. All that matters now is that you become my wife, and that we live out our days together."

"What?" She looked up at him wide-eyed.

"Marry me," he said quietly. "Be my lady."

"Well, when you put it like that, how can a woman resist?" she replied, smiling through her tears. "Can we go home now?"

He laughed and pulled her back in close, not wanting her to see the carnage that awaited them. He picked her up and cradled her in his arms, telling her to close her eyes as they walked through. When they emerged to the sunlight, he had the boys find a wagon in the Buchanan barn and hook two horses to it. He climbed inside, still cradling his love as they set course back to his home.

"Dougal," she said quietly as she leaned her head into him. "You know you can never leave this time."

"I will if it means staying with you."

"No, absolutely not," she said, shaking her head. "You are

the leader of this clan, and you must stay to allow the MacGavins to grow, to prosper, to produce heirs."

He started to say something, but she shook her head, placing a finger over his lips to silence him.

"I will stay with you," she said with a smile, as his heart filled with incredulity and the promise of everything he could have asked for. "This is your home, and I know this land well enough to understand it and appreciate it. I will write history with you, and ensure that it is written properly."

Dougal sealed her promise by kissing her soundly, leaving her no question as to his feeling toward her. He had enough self-restraint not to take her there in the middle of the wagon, but he wished he could urge the horses on faster, for he wasn't sure how much longer he could wait.

When they returned home, they greeted Arabel, who wept in relief at the sight of them, along with the others who stayed behind. Dougal gave Emilia just enough time to ensure them all she was fine, until he asked the girls to prepare her a bath and then whisked her to her bedroom. He wouldn't allow anyone but himself into the room as he helped her in the tub and grabbed a sponge, running it over her bruised but beautiful body. She leaned back against the edge and closed her eyes with a smile, which he imagined was from the scent of rose petals that had been added to the water.

Dougal ran the sponge over her breasts and down her stomach, getting hard as her naked body glimmered in the candlelight. She bit her bottom lip as he swirled the sponge right above her mound, moving back up to her breasts and down again. She shifted in the tub, spreading her legs apart and biting her bottom lip. He couldn't help the growl that pushed past his lips as he plunged the sponge back down under the water, this time running it gently over her core. She moaned softly as the water waved around her.

He dropped the sponge to the side and ran the same course, but this time with his bare hand. As his fingers parted her lips and rubbed against her very center, she flexed her hips slightly, inviting him in. He sat up against the edge of the tub and reached down deep, pushing two fingers now deep inside of her. She was warm and wet and he immediately needed to feel her wrapped around his shaft. He undressed in front of her, whispering wicked words to her as he removed his clothing. When he was completely naked, she pulled herself up to her knees, the hot water running over her body. She smiled as she leaned forward and fluttered her tongue over the tip of his manhood, sending chills up his spine as he sunk his hands into her hair.

She was the most sensual woman he had ever met, and she was entirely his. No one else, he thought fiercely, was ever going to touch her again.

He pulled her head back, leaned down, and kissed her pouty lips. He pushed her back in the tub and crawled in on top of her. The warm water washed over their bodies as he lifted her leg onto his shoulder, plunging into her in one swift motion. She moaned wildly as the water lapped against her, and he could feel her body tensing, letting him know she was already about to explode.

"Come for me lass," he groaned. "Come on, come for me."

She grabbed onto the sides of the tub as he rubbed his body up and down her. She arched her back and leaned her head behind her as the orgasm took hold. Dougal could feel her body stiffen as she tightened and vibrated against his shaft. He loved to watch her face as she let herself go to all of the sensations that he caused within her.

The warm burst around him sent heat down his legs and he grabbed onto her waist and pushed with his feet as he gyrated hard and deep inside of her. She gripped him tightly with her legs, calling out his name as he drove his hips down, hoping he wasn't hurting her but unable to stop. The sound of her moans and the throb of her around him was too much for him to handle and he began to move harder and faster now.

She moaned and drove her nails into his back as water splashed up and over the edges of the tub. As he pushed in one last time, he pulled her into him, holding his breath and feeling the waves of orgasm wash over him. His hips continued to move against her as he released everything he had been holding back for so long.

They slunk down in the tub together, letting the relaxation of the bath waters take over. As Dougal gripped her tightly in his arms, he was awash in the sensation that this incredible woman was going to be his wife. A forever that he could truly understand.

# EPILOGUE

It had been six months since Dougal and his clan had rescued her from the Buchanan's home. She had struggled for awhile with nightmares of the capture, from being taken to all she had heard while awaiting her fate, but having Dougal there beside her every night, taking her in his arms and kissing away the fear, made all the difference in the world. How very different and ugly war was when involved in it and not studying it in a book.

Emilia had taken one last trip back through the portal to straighten out her affairs and make sure the people she cared for the most weren't worried when she was gone. She told the dean that she had decided to move full time to Aberdeen. Her parents were each leading fulfilled lives with their new spouses and families, and she set things in motion to have regular letters and emails sent to them by a service she hired online. In them, she would try to slowly prepare and explain to them where she had gone. They might never fully understand, but at least she would have tried.

She stocked up on a healthy dose of toiletries and took half a day to stop at the library as well. She needed to check once more if the history books had changed, if she had forever disrupted the timeline with her travel back to the sixteenth century. She was again astonished to find that everything she knew remained unchanged, although already the description of the battle at Dunnottar Castle and the subsequent rise of the MacGavin Laird were much more detailed. Perhaps, then, this had always been predestined and her role was to simply describe the history as it occurred.

She had been fearful that when she stepped through the portal it would close behind her forever, so Dougal insisted on accompanying her. If they were trapped in the future, he promised, they would be trapped together.

On their return however, there it was, awaiting them. When they passed through and began walking away, it began to spark, and with a flourish crack in the air like the thunder all over again, it vanished completely. Emilia supposed she had done whatever it was the universe had planned for her. It was slightly unnerving to know now that she was here for the rest of her life with no option to return, but one look at Dougal's stoic face told her that she had made the right decision.

She and the girls had immediately begun planning her wedding. She was more than excited to live the traditions of the Highland Scottish and actually helped Arabel sew her wedding dress. When Arabel was done, she hung it up, one stitch left for Emilia to complete for good luck.

On the morning of the wedding, Emilia was nervous, to say the least, but the girls spent all morning primping and pruning her to look her best. They made sure to tie a bright blue ribbon around her thigh and put a penny in her shoe for good luck. Emilia sat there on the bed thinking about something old to have with her to complete the trifecta and she watched as Arabel came walking in the room, holding something in her hand. Emilia smiled at her as she opened her small palm, revealing a beautiful emerald bracelet.

"It was my mother's," she said, smiling wistfully. "Dougal gave it to me when she passed, and I should like to have ye wear it today. That way, you not only have something borrowed and old, yer allowing our mother to be part of this beautiful celebration of love."

"You are so wise," Emilia said, wiping a tear from her eye. "I would be honored to wear it."

She brought Arabel in close and squeezed her hard, loving her as she would have her own little sister. These children here had become her life, and she had Dougal to thank for that. When Emilia was completely dressed, she pinned the veil in her hair and pulled the lace front down over her face. Grasping the locket that had been returned to its place around her neck, she turned and stood before the smoky mirror, gazing in awe of her reflection.

She was marrying the Highlander she had spent her life studying. Who would have thought she would have literally jumped through her studies and into the pages of her history texts to take the man for herself?

She took a deep breath, hearing the bells signifying the beginning of the ceremony, and walked out to the edge of the porch. They were to be married in the property's small chapel. The doors opened to the grounds full of guests there to watch their leader marry his bride, the strange woman who they had all somehow come to accept.

The Highland background was absolutely stunning. Emilia gripped Ivor's arm, happy that he was there to walk her down the aisle. She was being given away by Ivor the Terrible. Unbelievable, she laughed to herself before turning serious as she caught Dougal's gaze on her from the front of the makeshift aisle. She could actually see a tear gathering in the corner of the proud warrior's eye.

They exchanged their vows and had the traditional knot tying ceremony, where they asked Arabel to join them together. As Emilia agreed to love and cherish this man forever, she looked up into his green eyes and smiled. Dougal slipped the ring on her finger and didn't wait for the preacher's cue. He grabbed Emilia around the waist and pulled her in tight, pressing his lips hard against hers.

Everyone cheered as Dougal bent Emilia backward and showed their love to the clan. From there they broke out into celebration, eating traditional food, drinking amazing brews, and dancing deep into the night. Emilia didn't know many of the dances but Dougal walked her through them, telling her that he would accept any excuse to hold her close. The laughter of the guests echoed across the fields and out over the cliffs, disappearing into the waves of the ocean. Their love had come full circle, and where Emilia had once been terrified and bewildered of her circumstance, she was now more excited than ever at what her life had to offer.

Near the end of the night, Emilia stood on the edge of the field, looking out at the moon and listening to the children dance to the Scottish tunes. Dougal walked up behind her and slid his hand around her waist, kissing her gently on the neck. Emilia took in a deep breath and sighed, knowing that she had been given a gift.

Emilia turned and looked at the party behind then, pausing for a moment and smiling at the now-familiar figure with her shock of red hair in the background, eating cheese and waving exuberantly at Emilia. She waved back and laughed, looking over at Dougal. He followed her eyes over, then back to her in confusion.

"Who are you waving at?"

"Just my fairy godmother," she said with a smile.

Dougal pulled her close and kissed her lips hard.

"Our story is one for the history books, wouldn't you say?" asked Emilia.

"I'm not sure anyone would believe it," he murmured into her lips.

"A fairy tale then," she said.

Fitting, it was. A fairy tale with a very happy ending.

\* \* \*

**THE END**

\* \* \*

Dear reader,

This series is something a little different for me, but I've always had a love of time travel. I wrote this series years ago but recently decided to revisit and rewrite it. It was like my own trip back in time to visit characters that I have always loved.

This book is a trilogy, with the third and final trip back in time taking place in A Time to Dream. Have you ever wondered what happens to the people the time traveller has left behind? The third book in the series explores that idea when Bryan goes looking for Emilia. There's a little teaser for you in the pages after this one, or you can head right to the Amazon page and download: A Time to Dream.

If you haven't yet signed up for my newsletter, I would love to have you join us! You will receive a free book as well as links to giveaways, sales, new releases, and stories about my coffee addiction, my struggle to keep my plants alive, and how much trouble one loveable wolf-lookalike dog can get into.

[www.elliestclair.com/ellies-newsletter](www.elliestclair.com/ellies-newsletter)

Or you can join my Facebook group, Ellie St. Clair's Ever Afters, and stay in touch daily.

Until next time, happy reading!

With love,
Ellie

\* \* \*

*A Time to Dream*
*To the Time of the Highlander Book 3*

**A person cannot simply disappear without a trace… or can they?**

While his former girlfriend may not have been his true love, Bryan Smith cannot shake the feeling there is more to her disappearance than what others have accepted. He sets out to her last known location of Stonehaven, Scotland to investigate, where his search leads him down a path he never thought possible – into the bedchamber of a 16th century woman.

Sorcha Singleir is desperately attempting to avoid the marriage her father has chosen for her, but sees no escape without bringing ruin to her clan. Until one night a handsome, mysterious stranger appears in her bedroom, potentially changing everything.

As Bryan and Sorcha work together to prevent her marriage, they cannot help but be drawn to one another – even though they know there is no future together. With all of the barriers between them, will they choose to love regardless, or put a stop to it before it can even begin?

# AN EXCERPT FROM A TIME TO DREAM

PRESENT DAY ~ NEW YORK CITY

The Internet contained more information than one could ever need, yet sometimes nothing at all that a person actually wanted.

Bryan cursed as his search through web pages associated with Stonehaven once again came up empty. No mention of Emilia Guthrie, Professor of History. He ran a hand through his hair, realizing he should probably shower.

He sighed. This made no sense at all. It had been six months since Emilia had left their home together, first leaving him, and then taking time away in the village of Stonehaven, Scotland. He'd then been shocked when he heard she had apparently given up the job of her dreams here at the University of New York, deciding to stay and make her home in the small Scottish town. Emilia was reasonable, and he couldn't believe she would make a sacrifice like that. He knew she loved Scotland and its history, but the position at the university would likely only come once in a lifetime. Had she found someone else in Scotland? He had to admit it hurt a bit to know she had gotten over him that quickly.

Although, if he was being truthful with himself, he supposed it wasn't a stretch. They hadn't exactly been the picture of togetherness at the end of their relationship. And once she had taken the step and moved out, he realized it had been for the best. They had become more roommates than lovers — friends, really, more than anything. He did feel badly, however, over the fight that had been the last straw.

When she had come home with the news that she had been offered the position of Dean of Scottish History at the university, he had lashed out at her in what he knew now had been a fit of jealousy, as he would have longed for a similar opportunity. He had worked for years for tenure in the philosophy department of the university, and despite numerous accolades from both his peers and the higher-ups, he was still waiting.

Did she receive the offer because of her connection to the former dean? Were there less applicants for her position? Or was it — he stopped himself. Or, maybe, it was because she deserved it.

He was proud he could finally admit that fact. He only wished he had been able to say that to her. He wanted to, now, and had tried getting in touch with her, only to continue to receive the same routine messages that she was out of service and would return his emails and phone calls shortly. When he did receive a response email, it didn't sound like her at all, but rather like an automated reply that anyone could have written.

He had begun to worry about her. This wasn't like Emilia. No, they were no longer romantically involved, but he still cared about her, and likely always would. He wanted to re-develop that friendship again, even if it was simply through emails back and forth.

Bryan had met Emilia in college, when she was a freshman and he was a sophomore. He knew that over the years his fascination with the great philosophers had begun to annoy Emilia, but he never thought she would actually leave. She hadn't understood his fascination with trying to find answers to the questions that nagged at him, the questions he wasn't sure if humankind would ever truly be able to understand. Although, to be fair, he hadn't understood her obsession with the past.

He had been angry for some time after she left. Eventually that anger turned to melancholy until finally he realized that she had been right. One of them should have left quite some time ago, but they had become too comfortable with one another, with the routine of daily life. No matter what happened, though, she would always remain one of his closest friends. She knew more about him than perhaps anyone else — his likes, dislikes, what set him off into a mood, and what calmed him down.

He knew that Emilia would never simply vanish to Scotland. She had emailed shortly after the trip ended, telling him how much she loved it there, and that she was staying. That was it. He knew they had not departed on good terms, but he was perplexed by the way she had completely cut off everyone from her former life.

So here he was now, just wanting to make sure she was all right. Her parents, whom she had never been close to, didn't seem to care much, and her friends, who were all married with children, seemed to have simply accepted the fact that Emilia left behind all she knew to extend her holiday into a new life.

He had to make sure she was all right. Until that happened, he didn't know if he could ever truly move on from her. He couldn't let this continue to nag at him, not knowing why she had chosen to stay or what had truly happened to her.

He took a sip of his coffee as he looked at all of her public profiles. Facebook — no update. Instagram — no update. He had sent off a short email earlier that morning asking her how she was, but hadn't been satisfied with the reply. "I'm very well, thanks, how are you?" was all it said. This wasn't her. Had she hired someone to look after her correspondence? And if so, why? He decided to respond, asking something that only she would know. He received a ping shortly after — "Why are you asking me this? You must move on, Bryan." He had moved on, damn it. He had no wish to be with her, he just wanted to make sure she was ok.

Back and forth the emails went, but hers could have been written by anyone. This was not Emilia. He knew it in his very bones.

He left the computer, downed the last of his black coffee, and placed his cup in the sink to wash later. He hadn't been much of a cook these past months and so rarely washed the dishes. Instead, it was a lot of takeout from Johnny's Pizza round the corner and Edo Japan. It meant he had more time to spend in the gym and out running, which was fine with him. It cleared his head and gave him time to think.

He changed and laced up his sneakers before heading out into the crisp early winter air of New York City. The last remaining leaves in Central Park were red and gold, those that remained on the sidewalk crinkling under his feet along with a few drifts of snow.

He was halfway through his run when he realized there was only one action he had left. He continued to mull it over as he kept up his steady jog. He'd worked up a good sweat by the time he finished his daily ten miles. He waved to the familiar runners he passed or met on the path. The city's marathon was coming up soon, but Bryan had never had a wish to compete. He used running to clear his mind and work problems through, so he never kept track of his pace or time. He knew his route, and let his body go into auto-pilot while his mind wandered.

By the time he neared his apartment building, he had come to terms with his decision. He would have to go to Scotland and see for himself that Emilia was all right. He knew he would look like the crazy ex-boyfriend, but he didn't see any other way he could allow himself to move on, without first knowing she was well and safe.

He let himself into his apartment with new resolve. He kicked off his sneakers, and grabbed a glass of water before sitting back down at his desk, opening up the laptop and heading to Expedia.

Luckily, being in New York City, he had access to ample international flights. Typing in Aberdeen, Scotland, he found a few flights leaving in the next week. He figured it would take a few days to make sure everything was looked after here. He booked the ticket without a return flight. He'd figure that out once he got there, as it would depend on how long it took him to find Emilia. He didn't feel it would take long to find one woman in a small area, but you never knew.

Bryan felt slightly uneasy about this whole situation. He was not a man who did much on impulse. It was part of the reason why he enjoyed philosophy – it gave him the freedom to truly ponder various aspects of life.

And now he was off to Scotland. Emilia had been infatuated with the country, particularly with its history of the Highlanders. They were always at war, fighting amongst themselves. What was the draw? Although, he had to admit to himself, he would have enjoyed living in a time where a man's woman listened to him and his desires, who would go along with what he thought and felt, and not leave him to go traipsing off to Scotland on a whim because she felt unsatisfied with her life.

Never one to trust his phone for something important like plane tickets, he printed them off, stapled them, and placed them in the satchel he'd carry on the plane. He resolved to give his apartment a good clean before he left as well. It was fairly bare, as he hadn't replaced anything Emilia had left with. She had just started to move out her things, and last he heard she had asked a friend to deal with divesting of her belongings.

He rose from his chair and began stripping off his clothes as he made his way to the bathroom for a shower. As he did so, he began making a mental list of everything he needed to do and pack before he left. Scotland, he thought with a rueful laugh, here I come.

* * *

Keep reading A Time to Dream!

## ALSO BY ELLIE ST. CLAIR

*To the Time of the Highlanders*
A Time to Wed
A Time to Love
A Time to Dream

*Reckless Rogues*
The Earls's Secret
The Viscount's Code
The Scholar's Key
The Lord's Compass
The Heir's Fortune

*The Remingtons of the Regency*
The Mystery of the Debonair Duke
The Secret of the Dashing Detective
The Clue of the Brilliant Bastard
The Quest of the Reclusive Rogue

*The Unconventional Ladies*
Lady of Mystery
Lady of Fortune
Lady of Providence
Lady of Charade

The Unconventional Ladies Box Set

*Thieves of Desire*
The Art of Stealing a Duke's Heart
A Jewel for the Taking
A Prize Worth Fighting For
Gambling for the Lost Lord's Love
Romance of a Robbery

Thieves of Desire Box Set

*The Bluestocking Scandals*
[Designs on a Duke](#)
[Inventing the Viscount](#)
[Discovering the Baron](#)
[The Valet Experiment](#)
[Writing the Rake](#)
[Risking the Detective](#)
[A Noble Excavation](#)
[A Gentleman of Mystery](#)

The Bluestocking Scandals Box Set: Books 1-4
The Bluestocking Scandals Box Set: Books 5-8

*Blooming Brides*
A Duke for Daisy
A Marquess for Marigold
An Earl for Iris
A Viscount for Violet

The Blooming Brides Box Set: Books 1-4

*Happily Ever After*

The Duke She Wished For
Someday Her Duke Will Come
Once Upon a Duke's Dream
He's a Duke, But I Love Him
Loved by the Viscount
Because the Earl Loved Me

Happily Ever After Box Set Books 1-3
Happily Ever After Box Set Books 4-6

*The Victorian Highlanders*
Duncan's Christmas - (prequel)
Callum's Vow
Finlay's Duty
Adam's Call
Roderick's Purpose
Peggy's Love

The Victorian Highlanders Box Set Books 1-5

*Searching Hearts*
Duke of Christmas (prequel)
Quest of Honor
Clue of Affection
Hearts of Trust
Hope of Romance
Promise of Redemption

Searching Hearts Box Set (Books 1-5)

*Standalones*

Always Your Love
The Stormswept Stowaway
A Touch of Temptation
Unmasking a Duke

*Christmas Books*
A Match Made at Christmas
A Match Made in Winter

Christmastide with His Countess
Her Christmas Wish
Merry Misrule
Duke of Christmas
Duncan's Christmas

For a full list of all of Ellie's books, please see www.elliestclair.com/books.

# ABOUT THE AUTHOR

Ellie has always loved reading, writing, and history. For many years she has written short stories, non-fiction, and has worked on her true love and passion -- romance novels.

In every era there is the chance for romance, and Ellie enjoys exploring many different time periods, cultures, and geographic locations. No matter when or where, love can always prevail. She has a particular soft spot for the bad boys of history, and loves a strong heroine in her stories.

Ellie and her husband love nothing more than spending time at home with their children and Husky cross. Ellie can typically be found at the lake in the summer, pushing the stroller all year round, and, of course, with her computer in her lap or a book in hand.

She also loves corresponding with readers, so be sure to contact her!

www.elliestclair.com
ellie@elliestclair.com

Ellie St. Clair's Ever Afters Facebook Group

Printed in Great Britain
by Amazon